PALM SPRINGS KING

CALIFORNIA SUITS, BOOK FIVE

CLAIRE MARTI

To everyone who pursues their dreams despite the odds. Trust yourself and never give up!

 as that a frickin' camel floating on a red-striped raft in his hotel's swimming pool? The shimmering aqua water tempted him to shuck his head-to-toe black clothes, dive in, and cool off already. To escape the gargantuan orange orb scorching the back of his neck. Austin Michaels squeezed his eyes shut and wiped the sweat from his forehead.

He cracked one eye open and sure enough, the pool contained nothing but water. Great, now he was hallucinating. Heat stroke?

All he wanted was to float on an enormous raft, crack an ice-cold beer, and call it a day. He'd been buried in spreadsheets since just after sunrise. He checked his over-sized divers watch--waterproof and perfect for the pool--and cursed.

Shit, shit, *shit*. He was late for his appointment with Mackenzie Banks, his new hire who would be running the hotel's spa and wellness programs. When she'd suggested they meet first thing in the morning to review her plans for their Labor Day grand opening, he'd countered with 3:00 p.m.

Now it was 3:19.

Meeting with his Spa Manager was important but his evil genius CEO––his big brother Ryan––always came first. And Ryan needed the financial reports pronto. What the hell had he been thinking when he'd decided to join Ryan and his three best friends on this wild ride opening a string of California luxury boutique hotels?

Simple answer––retired rockstars weren't in high demand, except for maybe at wealthy children's sweet 16 birthday parties. His resumé consisted of a high school diploma, a couple platinum alt-rock records, and a few years managing a popular bar in Manhattan. Oh yeah, and a six week hospitality course.

He shoved his hair out of his face and pivoted away from the alluring oasis and headed to the cocktail lounge. No choice but to soldier on and meet Mackenzie in person. Ryan claimed her world-renowned reputation ensured the hotel spa would be a huge success.

Because he needed all the help he could get, he sure hoped so. His master plan was to assemble a team of experts to make his General Manager role easier. Sure, he'd written songs that rocketed to #1 on the charts but crunching numbers and marketing luxury resorts weren't among his natural talents.

He strode toward the lounge entrance and plucked the drenched fabric of his t-shirt away from his chest. Time to start wearing different clothes. No way in hell would his customary jeans and t-shirt work here in Palm Springs. Too damn hot.

He yanked open the floor-to-ceiling accordion-style French glass doors into his comfort zone: the cocktail bar and lounge overlooking the main pool area. His eyes adjusted to the dim lighting, and he stifled a groan when the first blast of air-conditioning caressed his over-heated face.

Thank god the hotel had been a remodel and not a new build. Although electrical and HVAC weren't complete in many areas yet, he'd ensured that the main building, which housed the bar and a handful of the guest suites, had functioning air-conditioning.

"I'm over here, Mr. Michaels." A melodic voice called out.

Mr. Michaels? That was Ryan, not him. He strolled to the jade green leather booth.

He stopped short and sucked in a sharp inhale. Holy crap was Mackenzie stunning. He'd caught a glimpse of her at the Cypress Coast Ranch grand opening in Monterey a few weeks ago but up close?

Long, sleek reddish gold hair cascaded around toned shoulders and framed a delicate oval face. Her chin was lifted, and her full lips were pressed into a flat line. Enormous blue-green eyes fringed with thick dark lashes echoed the swimming pool's depth but not its invitation. More like the Rockefeller ice rink in winter––glacial.

He recovered and flashed his signature grin, designed to charm. "Hi Mackenzie, call me Austin."

"Hi Austin, it's nice to finally meet you in person. I go by Kenzie." Her mouth curved up a hint at the corners. Almost a smile.

Time to turn things around because her emphasis on "finally" revealed her annoyance. Although she was a yoga teacher, so shouldn't she be relaxed and easy-going? It wasn't like she was some corporate stiff who'd be bent out of shape by his tardiness. Or bury him in paperwork.

His jaw relaxed. "Sorry I'm late. I got stuck in spreadsheets and lost track of time. It's almost happy hour and I'm grabbing a beer. What can I get you?"

Her truly remarkable eyes narrowed a fraction. "I don't

drink, thank you. Did I misunderstand? I thought we had a staff meeting to review the plans for the spa and hotel opening?"

Oops. He should have figured--she created resort spas, so she probably subsisted on cucumber water and açai bowls. So far, he was not impressing Ms. Banks. Something about her made him want to try.

"We do have a meeting--sorry--the bar is one of the coolest places in the hotel. I figured we'd be more comfortable here. What can I get you? Fizzy water or soda?"

She ran her tongue around her teeth. "Fizzy water would be great. Thank you."

"Be right back." He placed his laptop computer on the polished charcoal gray table and strode to the refrigerator behind the long, curved marble-top bar.

He grabbed the sparkling water and an amber lager and rejoined her. He placed the bottle next to her laptop and an enormous binder with a neon pink label.

"No glasses yet. Is that okay?"

"Of course. I may work in ritzy spas and hotels, but I'm not fancy."

He downed a mouthful, savoring the icy brew. "Well, that's good news because I'm not the most formal guy."

"Okay, not formal and not fancy. Got it. So how would you like to proceed? I've made you a copy of my 90-day plan and the breakdown of my weekly implementation schedule. Should we start with that, or did you have an alternate agenda?"

He swallowed a groan. Was his role running this hotel going to be all plans and timetables? This transition from being Food and Beverage Manager for the three hotels they'd opened over the last year to being responsible for everything at one location chafed.

If only his world hadn't imploded in Rome. If only all his

dreams hadn't shattered on his band's final world tour. He'd be sitting around strumming his guitar with Liam and writing new songs.

No spreadsheets. No overseeing contractors and selecting drapes, for fuck's sake. And definitely no strait-laced employees wanting to breakdown every hour of the day in writing.

Kenzie cleared her throat. "Umm, Mr. Michaels…I mean Austin, I'm flexible. How would you like to start? It's already after 3:30 and we've got a lot to cover."

"Anything but numbers. Staffing, marketing, renovations, anything but finance. Please."

Her luscious pink lips twitched. He studied her face--she could have been a model--he should know, he'd dated enough of them when he'd been the lead singer of Black Velvet Machine. His ex-girlfriend in New York had been a supermodel.

Like his ex, Kenzie's face was perfectly symmetrical, with high, carved from diamond cheekbones, a small straight nose, and unusually wide eyes. But where Chantelle had always been contoured, glossy, and selfie-ready, Kenzie's face was bare.

"Got it. No numbers. I can work with that. So, I've got broad autonomy with Sanctuary Spa and its branding, right? I want to ensure we've got a coordinated plan moving forward."

"Correct. Lucas oversees the accounting for all the hotels and will continue until we hire someone. Ryan's assistant, Jon, comes out next month to help out. I'm handling the music venue."

"Music venue?" Her eyes widened.

"Yeah, music venue. Part of The Monroe's branding includes live music." One of his requirements when he'd agreed to run this hotel. Music flowed through his veins, even if he hadn't performed or written a single lyric in years.

A crease formed between her eyebrows. "I've opened several luxury spas and none of them have been connected to concert destinations. The type of clientele we're seeking might be expecting something very different. Don't you worry that a music venue might dissuade the potential guests who are coming here for a relaxing escape?"

The hairs on the back of his neck prickled. "The type of clientele?"

"Music venues tend to attract noisy party types. Not wealthy spa-goers." She shrugged.

Irritation flared, mirroring the searing heat outdoors. He'd already hammered out the details with Ryan, who also initially had concerns. Was he really going to have to explain himself again?

He held up a hand, determined not to reveal his frustration. "I wasn't planning on having a mini-Coachella at the hotel. That's already happening every year a few miles away. The Monroe is an homage to Old Hollywood and all the actors, singers, directors, and producers who escaped to Palm Springs back in the day. Frank Sinatra, Marilyn Monroe, Dean Martin, to name a few, all would sing for casual nights, and it was an enormous draw.

"So, the vision is acoustic sets under the stars, live music on certain nights during and after dinner, maybe dancing. Not rock concerts." He was done with those. At least as anything other than a spectator.

"Oh, okay, that makes sense. I misunderstood. Old Hollywood glamour is the ambiance here." She reached out and pressed a cool palm on his forearm. A jolt of energy shot up his arm and he met her gaze.

"No worries. If you pretend I wasn't late, I'll pretend you

like music." He looked down and shifted away from her on the smooth leather seat.

Maybe he didn't need to be so defensive—the woman wanted the spa to be a success and they'd hired her for her expertise. Her obvious preparation and passion for her job was something he could admire.

And maybe his showing up late on her first day hadn't helped.

She blinked slowly. "I like music, okay? You caught me off guard. I'm sorry, this heat is making me irritable."

"Well, we agree on the weather. Maybe we should have thought about this before we agreed to work here, right?"

Her lips curved up into a genuine smile. "Yeah, my best friend laughed at me about settling in the desert, but I couldn't pass up the opportunity. And this place is incredibly beautiful—the perfect location for a tranquil spa. At least most of the year. So, there's that."

Kenzie was more reserved than he'd expected. But he was used to dealing with his brother Ryan, who generally scared the shit out of people until he knew them. They'd always been opposites, but he could always help his serious brother lighten up. Maybe the uber-organized Ms. Banks would relax once she was comfortable?

"Okay, hit me with that 90-day plan. I can handle it."

She slid the laminated folder across the table to him.

Austin flipped through the pages, "It's color coded and has a table of contents."

"Isn't it great? I color code everything. And this way, with the table of contents, you won't have to search for anything." She rubbed her hands together.

He groaned. "Lucy, our wedding planner in Monterey, is also a big fan of the colored tabs. Charlie's even worse. Just please tell me you don't use stickers."

"Stickers?"

"Yeah. Charlie makes stickers and slaps them on everything. She and Ryan almost came to blows over it." He chuckled.

She gasped. "Blows?"

"Oh sorry, not real blows. Hey––no violence tolerated. It's just when Ryan and Charlie first met, they hated each other. Everything was a battle. I'm pretty sure she put a kitten sticker on his brand new laptop, and he lost it." He laughed again.

"Aha. And now they're engaged, right?"

"Yeah, they're getting married at the end of the month. She's the best thing to ever happen to him. He can get really uptight, and she's helped him lighten up."

"So, what does he help her do?"

"She says he's her safe haven. He loves her unconditionally. They used to bring out the worst in each other and now they bring out the best. But fair warning––arguing is foreplay for those two." He shrugged.

Now, his solemn brother was barely recognizable––all butterflies and flowers. Come to think of it, Ryan hadn't been the only one to catch feelings with another employee. Jack and Campbell fell for each other in Paso Robles and Cameron and Lucy had been reunited in Monterey. They'd joked about him being next.

A shiver of unease snaked down his spine. "I'm getting a water. Can I get you another bottle?" He rose and half-jogged to the bar. He needed some space––no way was he ending up engaged, like all the other Hotel Kings.

No way in hell.

"I'm fine."

Yes, yes you are. Not that he'd ever act on it. He scrubbed his hands through his hair and grabbed a bottle of ice-water. Time to tuck his emotions away and act like the boss.

CHAPTER 2

ime to practice what she preached to her yoga students: Kenzie released a long exhale and reminded herself the quickest way to soothe anxiety was to extend exhales twice as long as inhales. Vishama Vritti technique worked like a charm. If the nerves dancing along her skin were any indication, she'd be using the yogic skill designed to soothe the parasympathetic nervous system often around Austin.

As a yoga teacher, projecting serene strength was important, which meant mastering her emotions. Since patience wasn't one of her natural gifts, she worked extra hard to remain even keeled.

Even when she was screaming inside.

Somehow, within mere minutes in Austin Michaels' presence, he'd triggered the fiery nature she carefully controlled. Her belly had hopped, skipped, and jumped when he sauntered in looking more like the rock star he used to be. Stepping onto center stage, ready to unleash his signature raspy voice that had catapulted his band to the top of the alt-rock charts.

Rock and roll wasn't her thing but she hadn't lived on Mars. At the height of Black Velvet Machine's fame, his chiseled features, naughty grin, and tall, rangy frame had graced many a magazine cover. For a few years, the band was everywhere from Saturday Night Live to a Newsweek cover story on the second wave of alternative rock. What Pearl Jam and Soundgarden had embodied in the 90s, Austin's band represented in the 2010s. He'd drawn comparisons to the late Chris Cornell, whose posters she'd had plastered on her walls growing up, even if she hadn't listened to a lot of his music.

Yeah, Austin was her own personal brand of catnip and if she let her guard down, all her meticulously laid plans could implode. In person, her boss radiated charisma, especially in this close of quarters.

Austin slid back into the booth and picked up the folder again. His fingers were long, blunt, yet graceful. Like the guitar player he was. *Do not contemplate what those skilled hands could accomplish. Focus on something else, girl.*

A flash of heat sparked down her spine. Time to harness her reactions and this meeting. Controlling situations was her superpower. At least at work.

He glanced at the report and asked, "Are all yoga teachers so well-organized?"

"The good ones are. And teaching is only one of my roles. I specialize in creating world-renowned spas. My ability to coordinate, plan, and execute all aspects of the business is why you guys hired me." At least that's what she'd believed.

Organization was one of her top skills and had served her career well so far. Having a well-designed plan was essential for success. Even if her new boss didn't seem to believe it.

He raked his hand through his dense, almost shoulder-length hair——was it as silky and soft as it looked? When he leveled a stare at her, she realized his irises weren't dark brown.

Nope, they were a blue so deep as to appear almost black. The thicket of black lashes framing those gorgeous eyes added to the illusion. They were indigo, like the infinite depths of the ocean and about as profound.

Her entire future was riding on positioning Sanctuary Spa at The Monroe as one of the premiere spa destinations in the country. And unlike the other six now award-winning spas she'd opened from Bali to Switzerland to Maine, she wasn't cutting ties once it was launched. No, her dream was to not just build this spa but stay and run it, teach yoga, and plant roots in the desert.

If she could handle the heat, both outside and in.

So, she'd slip this unwelcome attraction to Mr. Rock Star Hottie deep in the vault. No way would Austin catch a glimpse of her untoward thoughts.

"Good to know." She cleared her throat and opened her folder. "Can you turn to page two please and we'll get started. Were you going to take some notes?" He hadn't opened his laptop.

"I thought you made them all for me already?"

"Very funny. At the end of the day, it's your hotel. This is my area of expertise but I'm open to suggestions. Now, I've got an extra highlighter if you want to mark any passages and I have sticky tabs." And yes, they were different colors. Neon colors.

"Sticky tabs? Aren't those stickers?" His dark brows lifted, and he caught his full lower lip between his teeth.

She reached into her satchel and pulled out the small pad of various colored stickies. "Not stickers, stickies. So, you can tab pages that you want to revisit? How else will you find them without wasting time?"

Austin rolled his eyes and flashed a grin. "I think the only time I've used tabs to mark pages was when I was signing contracts. But sure, why not? Can I have the bright blue and the traffic cone orange ones?"

"Absolutely. Blue for yes and orange for no?"

"Come again?"

"Well, you know, orange traffic cones mean to slow down or stop. Just figured you were using the imagery." And based on the expression on his beautiful face, he was quickly learning just how eccentric she could be. Oops.

He smirked. "Busted. That's exactly what I was doing. But maybe I should have picked green and red instead of blue and orange? You know, like the stoplights?"

Warmth flooded her cheeks. "No need to make fun of me. But I suggest that's how you use them. It's the most logical way. You ready?"

"Teasing, not making fun. It's part of the company culture––you good with that?" His smiled faded.

"Of course. But not all high-end hotel managers are so relaxed and easy-going." Not even close.

"Yeah, I bet. Don't get me wrong––I get things done and done right. But we're a more relaxed culture, more like family. Just tell me if I'm too much. You're in charge of the spa and I trust your judgment but at the end of the day, I need to sign off on everything."

Why did his voice have to have that husky quality, like he'd overused it last night or something? Even when he was speaking, his voice was hypnotic. Add that onto the hint of mischief dancing in his eyes, and his clean woodsy scent, and she'd need to be vigilant to avoid falling under his spell. Acquiescing to his sheer sex appeal would be too easy.

Not that he'd acted inappropriately but she'd seen his eyes widen and gleam with appreciation when he arrived. No, no, no, no. Austin Michaels was her boss, and her type. One role was appropriate and the other not so much.

"Of course. Let's go ahead and start with the staffing. If we hire the best massage therapists and estheticians, we'll be golden. Are you okay with me setting up test massages and facials for us?"

His eyes widened. "You want me to get a facial?"

"Yes, and a massage. Come on, you've gotten massages before, right? And didn't you ever receive facials before some of your appearances?"

Not one of his thick black lashes flickered but his lips tightened a fraction before he replied. "Massages, of course. Facials, nope."

"You said Jon will be out, right? I can recruit him, but I think you deserve the pampering. Facials are really relaxing and rejuvenating. You'll love it. Besides, the air is different here. You'll need a different skincare regime to combat the desert climate. What better way to get started, right?"

He barked out a laugh. "Okay, okay. I'll be a guinea pig, but no way is anybody waxing my eyebrows."

She grinned. "Deal, your eyebrows remain in their virgin state. Otherwise, I won't have a face left if I test out all the candidates. I'll make sure to coordinate some auditions when Jon is here, too."

"He'll be all over free pampering. Okay, so you've got the budgets and are comfortable ordering all the equipment for the yoga and workout studios, the spa supplies?"

"Yes, everything from start to finish--that's my specialty. If something threatens to exceed the budget, how do I handle that?"

A crease formed between his thick brows. "You think you're going to exceed the budget? The spa is already one of the hotel's highest expenditures. We can't take away from the restaurant we're planning to put on track for a Michelin Star restaurant or the music venue."

"No, I don't think so, but you never know what can

happen. And I'm still concerned about this music space being counter to the Zen vibes we need." She threaded her fingers together in her lap, her nails digging into her palms.

Austin crossed his arms and leaned back into the booth. She did her best not to ogle his tanned forearms. Lean muscles and prominent veins with a light sprinkling of dark hair could serve as cover-arms for Forearm Porn Magazine, should such a publication exist.

Rule number one of negotiations was that the first person who spoke, lost. So, she'd wait and see what he said. But her gut screamed that the music venue could throw a serious wrench into her detailed plans.

He leaned those gorgeous forearms onto the table's edge and pinned her with his gaze. "Look, Kenzie. I hear what you're saying but I don't think you understand my vision. It will complement the spa. We can look at ways to coordinate some music events that will be unique to Sanctuary. But it's going to happen. If you think you cannot open the spa and co-exist with the music aspect of this resort, then maybe this isn't the place for you."

So much for the magic negotiation rule. "I didn't mean that, but I just can't help expressing how I feel. And I'm happy to discuss some music and spa events. What do you suggest?"

"How about I grab my guitar and we head out to the area, it's part of the patio section of the restaurant. I'll play a few acoustic songs and give you an idea of what I'm thinking. Deal?"

"Okay, that works. And the restaurant and patio are on the opposite side of the resort from the spa. That makes more sense." Maybe she'd been jumping to conclusions for no reason. Austin unsettled her.

He nodded, his voice impassive. "It's still too hot for me

but why don't we finish reviewing your plans and we'll meet there at 7:30. Okay?"

"Absolutely. Well, let's move on to the sauna and steam room build-outs."

He laughed, and just like that, they were back on friendly ground. "Why anyone would want to go into a sauna in this weather is beyond me but lead on."

Yeah, the desert temperatures weren't the only flames scorching her world right now.

Mr. Austin "Forearms" Michaels was more than she'd bargained for.

CHAPTER 3

*K*enzie smoothed down her soft cotton maxi-sundress and wrestled with the nerves fluttering in her throat. The reality was she was about to sit with one of the most famous lead singers of the past decade while he played the guitar as the sun sank over the mountains.

She couldn't kid herself——the minute he'd sauntered over to the booth, easy as you please——a visceral jolt of energy had bloomed low in her belly. A powerful awareness she was teetering on shaky ground filled her.

One: Austin Michaels was her boss. The Monroe was her home for the foreseeable future. In other words, the old cliché, no fishing in the company pond, applied.

Two: Austin Michaels was her type. Correction, her *former* type——charismatic bad boy. After Jason and Scott and——she shook herself back to the present.

No time to reminisce about her history of questionable relationship choices.

If the universe had conspired to create the ultimate kryptonite for her it would be the lean, rangy, sexy as hell man with whom she'd spent the afternoon.

Austin was a classic bad boy. Rebellious teen. Tortured rockstar. Had the requisite motorcycle and black leather jacket. Reformed--maybe? She didn't do bad boys anymore. Especially ones with whom she worked.

Relationships could come later. With a stable, sweet man--the kind referred to as cinnamon roll heroes in her favorite romance novels.

Handsome, but not dangerously handsome.

Assertive, but not aggressive.

Successful, but not famous or obnoxiously wealthy.

Confident, but not arrogant.

Safe, but not boring. That guy had to exist in the real world, right?

Austin Michaels was no cinnamon roll. He was more of a triple scoop of Nutella gelato or a decadent devil's food cake. And she'd been scorched by his type before.

Tonight was business. Making her dream a reality by implementing her two-year plan to

create another world-renowned spa where she could build a future.

She patted on some sheer lip gloss, slid on her sparkly gold flip-flops, and hurried outside. After giving him attitude about being late today, she needed to be on time.

The minute she left her air-conditioned room, the crisp desert air caressed her skin. Now the sun was setting, the temperature had dropped, and it was lovely. The night sky was a dusky blue with streaky fingers of cotton-candy clouds. The sun sat heavy over the rocky mountain range, coloring the sky in deeper tones of violet and indigo.

She traversed along the stone pavers past free-standing suites with interiors in various stages of remodeling--some completed, others still shells.

Although she was accustomed to mountains with dense evergreens and varied foliage, the reddish rocky mountains framing Palm Springs evoked a unique beauty. The sprinkle of lights ahead signaled the large semi-circle patio area Austin wanted to use for concerts. Or acoustic music. It sat right outside of the floor-to-ceiling glass doors framing the restaurant.

A clanking noise sounded, and she spotted Austin fiddling with a couple folding chairs.

He glanced up and flashed her a crooked grin. "I realized we don't have the outdoor furniture yet, so I grabbed these from the storage space."

Nerves danced along her spine and she returned his smile. "We'll make sure not to take any photos. Imagine these being leaked online. Hotel Kings next luxury boutique hotel not so luxurious."

He chuckled. "Definitely no pics. We're a work-in-progress, for sure. I grabbed us a couple waters. Have a seat." He swept one arm with a flourish toward the white plastic seat, like it was a royal throne.

Once again, he wore black, the t-shirt showing off the sinewy muscles of his arms and highlighting his lean frame. He sat down and laid his guitar across his long denim-clad legs. His dark hair was damp, a few pieces waving around his gorgeous face. If someone took a portrait, they could call it "Beautiful Rockstar." It could be part of the spread on his cover story for Forearm Porn from earlier today.

Time to start talking business and stop ogling him. She sank into the stiff chair and folded her hands in her lap. "Okay, so this venue is amazing. What are you thinking?"

"Well, it depends. We'll have furniture set up with happy hour in mind but also have it as overflow seating for the restaurant. The musician or trio can sit here." He waved an arm. "We can tweak it depending upon the use. If we want dancing in the evenings, that's an option as well. In other words, it's flexible."

"So, in the evenings, a musician could play acoustic music during dinner or afterwards?"

His long fingers drummed on his guitar. "Yeah. And acoustic is a given."

Maybe she'd overreacted earlier. Part of it had been her irritation at his tardiness but she was also so fixated on making Sanctuary Spa a success, that anything outside of her careful plans stressed her out. Yeah, not so Zen, but she was working on it.

"Sounds good." Getting along with her boss wasn't optional. "Play something like what you're suggesting."

He picked up his guitar and adjusted it across his thighs. "Hmmm, I've got one for you. Let me know what you think."

His gaze shifted to the guitar strings, his full lower lip caught between straight white teeth. He strummed a few chords before tender notes floated up into the warm evening air, immediately causing her heart to catch. He hummed along but didn't break out his signature vocals.

Every muscle in her body softened and she sank deeper into the chair, the unyielding discomfort of the plastic fading away. The haunting melody permeated her being. Her eyes drifted closed and all she could do was savor the beauty Austin was creating.

Intense emotions crowded her chest until her heart felt close to bursting and liquid pooled behind her eyelids. She squeezed her eyes tighter to prevent tears from dripping down her cheeks.

He finished the song, the last note lingering in the gentle breeze.

When she opened her eyes, he sat in a position of almost supplication, both hands on his guitar, his eyes closed, his chiseled lips pressed into a flat line. Yeah, he'd made her feel instantly but at what cost to him? Obviously, the song was intensely personal.

She exhaled and leaned forward. "Austin?"

His head jerked upward, and his eyes flew open. He'd been a million miles away.

When he didn't respond, she tried again. "Do you want to talk about it? I'm a good listener."

"It's not a happy story."

"That came across. But sometimes nothing beats sharing it with someone. Especially someone objective."

Wanting to help others was as natural to her as breathing. Although she'd conquered her tendency to try to fix people, she had honed her ability to listen since she started teaching yoga.

"You're objective?" One dark brow quirked.

"Well, we just met today. We don't know each other. Maybe I can offer a fresh perspective?" Although judging by the song, she might just be inviting him to tell her about a lost love or his ex-girlfriend.

But too late now. Suddenly it seemed urgent she help him release some of the pain etched across his features.

"It's not like it isn't public knowledge." He carefully set the guitar down next to him and shoved his hair back from his face. "But maybe you're right. This is between you and me though, yeah?"

"Of course. I'll lock it up in the vault." She pursed her lips and mimicked turning a key and tossing it over her shoulder.

One corner of his gorgeous mouth lifted. "Okay, Ms. Mackenzie Banks, the vault it is. But you have to share something personal with me too, okay?"

Crap, what had she just agreed to? Because her upbringing was not something she divulged to anyone. "That sounds fair. I've got plenty of unhappy stories, but I've never been able to release them by creating pure beauty, like you do."

He crossed one leg across the other. "I wrote that song the

week after my best friend Tommy died. I couldn't process everything I was feeling. Hell, I still haven't processed it."

"Oh Austin, that's terrible. Was this recent?"

His eyes widened. "It's been almost three years. You really didn't read about it?"

"Three years ago, I was in the Maldives, which is really removed. I was immersed in designing the spa for a new 5-star resort there. I didn't keep up with much news."

Of course, she'd heard the band had broken up, but she hadn't read the details. Maybe she should have googled Austin, but his fame hadn't interested her. Her research had been focused on the Hotel Kings LLC, not her new boss's celebrity status.

He shrugged. "Okay. Well, touring was intense. We loved it but the pressure of putting on an incredible show night after night, and then repeating it while traveling around the world gets to you. Partying after a concert was a way to come down but it's easy to get caught up.

"Tommy started experimenting with harder drugs and spiraled fast. We were in Tokyo and were playing a two night gig. We didn't have a day off in between arriving in Tokyo from Sydney and I think Tommy amped himself up to play and then took some sleeping pills because he couldn't relax."

He paused and looked down, his strong jaw clenched, his long eyelashes fanning out on his cheek.

"Austin, you don't have to keep going. I get the picture. I'm so sorry." The minute he mentioned the addiction, it triggered memories of her alcoholic parents. Both out of control, but in different ways. Oh, she empathized with the helplessness and despair.

He turned back to her, his eyes bleak. "Nah, I'll finish it. I crashed after the show and in the morning when we headed down to breakfast, Tommy didn't join us. That wasn't unusual but then it was time for our limo to take us to the airport and he still hadn't come out of his room. He wasn't answering, so we had to have hotel management unlock the door."

He dropped his head in his hands and paused again. The raw pain radiated off him in waves.

Her stomach knotted into ropes, and she reached across and stroked his shoulder. Desperate to offer comfort. "Austin--"

He continued as if she hadn't spoken. "It was a nightmare. He was face down on the bed. He'd been dead for hours. They ruled it an accidental overdose. He was my best friend and we lost him halfway around the world."

She blinked back the moisture in her eyes. "I'm so sorry. That's terrible. Did writing the song help?" Grief was a difficult beast with no timeline and no rhyme or reason.

"A little bit. Bleeding on the page and all that. But sometimes I miss him so damn much." The raw vulnerability in his deep voice pierced her heart.

"I can only imagine. I've never lost someone close to me before." And she was an expert at keeping most people at arm's length. Up until her decision to start fresh and build a life in one place, she'd found it easier. Even her handful of friends were scattered around the world.

"You're lucky. It's not uncommon in my world. And that's part of the reason I'm here now, working with my brother."

"Did the band break up after that?"

"Well, I told them I was done. The other guys wanted to keep going but I couldn't. I couldn't keep going without Tommy. So here I am."

And now his insistence on the music venue made total sense. Music was an integral part of his soul. But judging by the suffering emanating from him when he played, his body was still full of pain. Losses like that could haunt a person for a lifetime.

"I understand. Sometimes a clean break is the only way to move forward. And I get how vital having music here is for you now. I think this can work, especially if it's after dinner and the spa will be closed."

He gave a small smile. "Thanks. Okay, that was probably TMI, especially on your first day. But I'm a good listener too, so it's your turn."

She bit her lip. "We're keeping this private, right?" Now that he'd shared such an intimate loss with her, he deserved something real from her.

"Of course."

"So, I have a really difficult relationship with my mother." Definitely an understatement, but it was the truth. And no way would she share about both her parents. Too much too soon.

Austin's brows knit together over his strong straight nose. "Difficult how?"

She lifted her eyes skyward and contemplated the deepening horizon, the purple streaks from earlier now engulfed in black. The night sky illuminated the brilliance of the stars, poking through the dark like sparkling diamonds.

"Have you ever been around narcissists?"

He barked out a laugh. "Umm, rock musician, remember? It's more common for musicians to be narcissistic than not. Your mom is one?"

"Yeah, after years of research and therapy, I learned the true term is victim narcissist. Every problem in her life was caused by others, never herself. And everything in her life revolved around her. I got a good grade? It's because I inherited her intelligence. I did something stupid, like getting caught skipping school? It's because I was trying to hurt her. You get the picture."

"That's tough, especially as a kid. What about your dad?"

"He's another story for a different day and I don't see

them often. They live in Florida. My mother calls occasionally and I can't seem to completely cut her off, but I haven't seen either of them in almost six years." Not that she was counting.

"I'm sorry, that's rough. Well, some people end up incredibly successful despite their upbringing and you seem to be one of them."

"We all have a story, right? We can't choose our family of origin, but we can choose to move forward from whatever cards we were dealt and create a life we want. Sometimes I think my ambition comes from wanting to prove them wrong."

She'd managed to do it in her career. Now to see if she could replicate her success and get a healthy personal life. At least not turn out like her parents.

His lips curved up. "I hear you on that. Thanks for sharing. I've got some things to take care of tonight. So, are we good with the music?"

"We're good." She couldn't deny it was beautiful and if it was mellow, it could be a powerful complement to evening events at the resort. And maybe they could offer some themed yoga classes with live music. But she'd save that concept for another time.

An idea popped into her mind, and she blurted it out before she could think better of it. "Hey, do you want to practice some yoga with me in the morning? It's a great way to balance out stress." To release pain. It would help him let go of that unprocessed emotion he was clinging to.

He narrowed his eyes. "I can't touch my toes or stand in some kind of cactus pose."

She laughed. "You mean Tree pose? And that's why you practice yoga, to become more flexible and balanced and strong."

"I've got a really busy day tomorrow." He stood, picking up his guitar.

"Well, I practice every morning. And just like you showed me how the music venue would work, I think if you got into a regular yoga practice, it would help enhance your ability to promote the spa."

Although seeing him moving and stretching might be too much eye candy for her to handle, especially after his trusting her with his story tonight.

"Huh. We'll see. I'm going to head back in. You coming or hanging out here a little longer?"

A little fresh air was what she needed. Without his intoxicating presence. "I think I'll hang out for a bit and meditate. It's peaceful out here."

"Enjoy that. G'night." He gave a quick wave, pivoted on his heel, and sauntered away. And she was absolutely not checking out his very sexy butt.

She closed her eyes and leaned her head back. Yeah, the odds of her dropping into a focused meditation were not in her favor. Austin Michaels wasn't just a pretty face; he had some serious depths. A sensitive artistic soul that pulled at her. Hard.

She'd revealed more to him about her mother than she had with most people. And she got the feeling he didn't go around disclosing the story of losing his best friend and band mate.

No, they'd shared intimate details on her first day of work. Not scary at all. She'd need to be careful and maintain her boundaries around him or jeopardize the dream life she had planned.

CHAPTER 4

"Hey, you still there?" Ryan asked.

"Sorry, I've got a lot on my mind. Things are moving along, despite this freakin' weather. Thank god we listened to Craig and finished the new roof and exterior paint before summer arrived."

But the fact nobody wanted to work outdoor construction when the temperatures averaged 111 wasn't why he was distracted. Last night hadn't exactly been a restful one. Kenzie's soft eyes when he'd shared about Tommy and the set to her jaw when she'd matter-of-factly described her mom haunted him.

Last night they'd shared a moment. Many moments. It was one thing to think she was hot. But discovering the well of resilience and kindness beneath her polished exterior? Dangerous. Time to get a grip, pronto. No way in hell could he afford to be attracted to his new spa manager.

Austin shoved away from his desk and stalked to the wall of windows in his suite. Today the sun was once again relentless in the brilliant blue bowl of a sky.

"I'll be coming out with Jon next month to help out. Lucas

is planning on coming out too. You haven't changed your mind about staying in Palm Springs?" Ryan's curt tone snapped him back to the present.

And there it was––Ryan expecting him to flake out. It was his older brother's job to ensure that all the Hotel King's locations were running smoothly, but sometimes Ryan still treated him like his black sheep baby brother.

He gritted his teeth. "No, I haven't changed my mind. I've been all in since we started this venture last year."

"I'm not questioning your commitment. But I know the desert is intense in the summer. Maybe Jon will change your mind. For some reason, he likes it hotter and says he can't wait to lounge in the pool all day."

Austin chuckled. "Yeah, he can hang with the lizards, snakes, and camels."

"Camels? You're not in Egypt, bro."

A few years back, he'd ridden a camel in Cairo and hadn't been a fan of the foul-breathed, surly creature. Yeah, he knew there weren't any camels in Southern California, but he wouldn't be surprised if one ambled into The Monroe's new lobby and bellowed at the concierge.

"I know but something about this place…" He shook his head. "Kenzie will have Jon working his butt off completing her color-coded to-do list. He'll be lucky to make it to the pool by midnight."

"Kenzie? That was my next question, how's everything going? Does she have you in line yet?" Ryan's smirk relayed through the phone.

"Stick to your CEO gig, comedy isn't your forte." He ran his tongue around his teeth. "Yeah, she prefers Kenzie. Let's just say I expected her to be a little more relaxed and flexible, with her being a yoga teacher. The woman is pretty black and white."

Ryan hissed. "You didn't scare her off, did you? We need

her for The Monroe. Even though we've got our unique old Hollywood vibe, destination spa competition is fierce. She's the best in the industry."

"No, I didn't. You must mean the other way around. You remember that second grade teacher, Mrs. Williams, at our elementary school? The one who made us reorganize the crayons every single time we put them back in the container? Well, Kenzie makes that woman look sloppy." And why did her ridiculous attention to detail seem charming now?

Ryan barked out a laugh. "Oh my god, isn't she the one who called Mom when you were the third Michaels boy in her class? Asking for reassurance you'd be the last?"

"Yeah, that's the one. I think Grant almost drove her to retire early with his little Polaroid camera. And look at him now." Their brother was one of the top adventure sport photographers in the world.

"Yeah, when Charlie and I interviewed Mackenzie, she had binders with her. Charlie was thrilled to find a kindred soul. But it's a good thing, right? She gets stuff done."

"We'll see. We did have a little disagreement over the music venue." Austin rubbed the tight cords on the back of his neck.

"Hmm…you know I had some reservations too. But I trust you to make this work and I'm not going to interfere. Did you resolve her concerns?"

"Yeah, I think we're good. And remember, when the Hollywood elite used to come here back in the day, there was plenty of singing. Once I told her it would be more acoustic under the stars as opposed to Heavy Metal Rock Legends world tour, she relaxed."

Ryan snorted. "I like your idea and I think it will be a big draw, especially with you playing some sets. Hell, Charlie and I are so grateful you're going to play our first dance song at the wedding."

Austin's lips curved up. His brother had been devastated for him when he'd quit the band after Tommy died. Ryan had never wanted either of his little brothers to feel pressured to do anything except follow their passions. When their police officer dad had been killed in the line of duty when Austin had only been nine years old, Ryan had turned more into a father figure.

Even though Ryan had been only thirteen, he'd had to grow up fast. Once their mom got remarried to Chris McNeill after going to manage his household at Pacific Vista Ranch, the hotshot movie director had stepped in as a positive role model for him and his brothers.

"Thanks and I'm happy to play at the reception. I can just do what I'm good at and Jack will handle best man duty."

"You got all the music talent in the family and the guests are really lucky to have the perk of seeing the one and only Austin Michaels play."

"Okay, you're laying it on a little thick. What do you need me to do? Nothing for the wedding, I hope?"

"Hey, you know I think you're an incredible singer. And in terms of what I need you to do? Stay focused, don't piss off our spa guru, and ask for help if you need it. But yeah, make sure Jack doesn't plan anything over the top for my bachelor party. No strippers."

Austin rolled his eyes. "As if I could control Jack. And I don't need––"

"We all need help. I couldn't have gotten Pacific Jewel Inn going without you guys. We all helped Jack and Cam when it was their turn. We'll help Lucas in Beverly Hills. That's how it works. We're a team. If we're going to pull off another perfect opening like we did with the first few locations, we'll all play a part."

"Yeah, but now you guys have your own hotels to run. I don't want to slow anybody down." He needed to prove to all of them he was an equal. That he could hold his own, even if he lacked their corporate experience. Just because he didn't have all the fancy initials after his name didn't mean he wasn't smart. He'd graduated from the school of life. And another cliché.

Ryan's deep voice softened. "Don't worry about that. We agreed to this at the beginning. The better we work together, the better for all the locations and our brand, okay?"

"Yeah."

"And Austin, I mean it about Jack and my party." Ryan was using his *don't fuck with me* voice that usually had people shaking in their shoes. Too bad he was immune to it.

He smirked. "You should have Charlie keep him in line. Nobody wants to get on your fiancée's bad side. And I'll see if I can put a leash on Jack, but that's like trying to herd cats."

All he knew was Jack had asked him to use his connections to reserve private tables at a few Hollywood hotspots. Like he had time to party for twenty-four hours with the hotel opening a few months away. But seeing his serious brother let loose and have fun with the guys would be worth it.

They hung up and he tossed the phone back on his desk and paced back to the window. Time to prioritize. He had meetings with the drywall subcontractor, a Zoom call with Lucas to review more budgeting details––would that shit ever end? Because if he didn't have to crunch another number again, he'd die a happy man. Numbers had always challenged him, from hating math the first day he'd stepped into Geometry class until now. His weakest link for this job.

But damned if he would admit it. So what if it took him twice as long to get the reports put together? Nobody needed to know, and he wasn't afraid of hard work. But those extra hours sure seemed like a waste of time. For now, he'd suck it up. Cost of doing business and all that. He couldn't wait until Lucas came out and they hired a few finance peeps.

But he didn't have to like it. Hell, maybe Kenzie was right, and he needed some yoga and meditation. Maybe he could get all Zen over numbers.

He snorted and surveyed his room. He was staying in one of the master suites that came equipped with a full living area, including a dark charcoal teak desk that matched the other furniture.

The white walls and taupe tiled floors created a sense of cool crispness. White bedding added to the effect, as did the enormous floor-to-ceiling windows that invited in the San Jacinto mountains on the horizon and the meager shade of soaring palm trees. Framed black and white movie posters would grace the walls and each suite had a different "star" theme.

He was staying in the Sinatra suite and Kenzie was in the Reynolds for Debbie Reynolds. In addition to the glamorous décor and lavish furnishings, guests would be thrilled with the way each room's windows showcased the rugged Palm Springs terrain.

And air-conditioning. Blessed air-conditioning. The suites all featured modern fireplaces and although he knew the winter nights grew cold in the desert, right now, they seemed a ridiculous addition. But they'd done their research with other 5-Star desert hotels around the world and fire-places were the thing.

His ringtone sounded, and he stiffened when he saw the number flash on his screen. Liam. After Tommy died, he'd separated himself from his former lead guitarist and the rest of the band. He'd figured Liam would have given up reaching out by now.

The call ended and he exhaled and sank back into his chair. Yeah, maybe he was a coward but what was there to say? Instead of bonding over losing their friend and drummer, the guys had splintered apart.

Liam and Ben had wanted to just move along, to start recording and touring again, like nothing had happened. Fuck that. He'd needed to mourn his best friend.

A few months back, the group's former manager had notified him Liam was auditioning lead singers. At first, he'd wavered, but he'd made his choice never to return. He and Tommy had founded Black Velvet Machine--how could it ever be the same without them? Would the fans care? Hell, Axl Rose had assembled an entirely new band with Guns N'Roses for a decade--maybe not.

He stiffened when someone banged on the door. Was he late for something again? He rose and crossed the room, schooling his expression. When he opened the door, his jaw dropped.

His mouth snapped closed so hard it was a miracle he didn't shatter his teeth. "Liam? What are you doing here?"

"Mate, you kept blowing off my calls and we need to talk. How the hell are you?" His former guitarist's Manchester British accent hadn't softened with time. And the guy looked exactly the same--tall, lean, with a mop of curly blond hair women had lost their minds over.

"You came all the way to Palm Springs to ask me how I am?" His gut clenched. Liam wouldn't show up out here uninvited unless it was serious.

Liam sauntered into the suite and threw himself down on one of the loveseats. "I've been hanging out with some friends since last month. We were here for Coachella, and it was fuckin' brilliant. Did you see that I played with the Silver Smokers? Did you go?"

Coachella? Was he kidding with this? He hadn't been to a festival or big concert in more than three years. "No, didn't make it. How'd it go?" Austin closed the door and returned to his seat. His old friend was stubborn and wouldn't leave until he'd gotten what he came for––whatever that might be.

"Brilliant, like I said. Loved being back in the mix. And they headlined Saturday night, so it was huge. The crowds, the chicks, the buzz was off the charts. Everyone asked when we're putting out another record." His bottle green eyes narrowed.

Austin's fingers curled around his chair's arms. "You've got a new singer?"

"No, mate. That's why I'm here. We don't want a new singer. We want you. You got to come back. The fans. The execs. They're begging for us." He dropped his elbows on his legs and leaned forward, his jaw tight.

Well, apparently it was the day for tough discussions.

Austin's gut tightened and his pulse hammered in his temples. "No."

Liam's nostrils flared. "Come on, mate. You've got to be sick of playing this corporate gig. I know running the bar was fun for a spell, but it's been three years."

"I know exactly how long it's been." He could probably call it to the minute. Ironic he couldn't forget *those* numbers. "The Monroe opens in September and I'm on board. It's what I want to do."

Liam huffed a breath. "Seriously man? You're only thirty years old. You can't be giving it all up to be a pencil pusher."

And this is why he'd avoided Liam's calls. Tact wasn't in the guy's DNA. "I like what I'm doing." Mostly.

Liam surged off the couch and stalked toward him. "Bullshit. You're a musician. You're a fuckin' poet. You're one of a kind. I know you took losing Tommy hard, but he's gone. Do you think your best mate would want you to hang it all up? No way. He'd want you to do what you were put on this fuckin' planet to do. Write music. Play music. Let's get the band back together."

Austin ground his molars together. "I told you then and I'll tell you now, you need to find another lead singer. There're great people out there who'd kill to front the band. I'm not coming back."

Liam released a string of curses that made even Austin's eyebrows raise. He'd forgotten how rough around the edges the guy could be. Even though Liam was super-intelligent and had gone to law school in London, he often sounded like he'd been born behind a pub.

For a few moments, neither spoke. The kick of the air-conditioner in the suite flickered as white noise. His own breath was harsh, like he'd hiked the damn mountain outside his window.

"Look man, I'm not trying to be a dick, but my heart isn't in it, okay? I can't do anything halfway and I just cannot do it. You've got to let it go. Move on, okay?"

"Your heart isn't in it because you're running away. We've all been doing gigs with other bands but it isn't the same. You get back in the studio with us and it will all come back. We found an amazing drummer––he's not Tommy––but nobody is or will be again. Why don't you come out to L.A. for the weekend? Just hang out?" Liam's voice cracked–– betraying the depth of his emotions.

Nausea roiled in his gut. "I'm sorry, man, I'm not ready to hang out. And I've got a meeting I can't be late for."

Liam's face hardened and eyes chilled to chips of green glass. "Yeah, sure. Well, I guess I'll be in touch with the legal shit because Black Velvet Machine will go on with or without you. Never thought you'd be such a fuckin' coward." He pivoted, strode out the door, and slammed it behind him.

Damn it. The band had been his family. They'd spent more time together in a decade than most families linked by blood. He'd belonged with them and now he couldn't go back. Now he wasn't sure if belonged as one of the Hotel

King executives, but they were his family too and he had to try.

He crossed to the bathroom and flipped on the shower. Time to let the powerful torrents of water hammer down on him and help him wash away the guilt.

Guilt from letting down the guys in Black Velvet Machine, even though he'd had to save himself. Yeah, he'd hurt them, and he missed the friendships but at the end of the day, the environment was toxic for him.

Guilt even contemplating bailing on Ryan and the rest of the Hotel King crew. He'd known Jack, Cam, and Lucas since Ryan had gone to college with them. In a way, they'd been honorary big brothers. No way could he screw them over. Even if he'd gone from rockstar to rookie.

Over the last year, he'd loved being part of the tight-knit group. And he'd spent a great deal of time making sure he wasn't just Ryan's baby brother they'd allowed in as a favor.

He tossed his clothes into a heap on the floor and stepped into the already steamy shower. Pulsating jets massaged the tense muscles in his back and neck.

Damn it––although part of him yearned for the band days, he pushed it deep into the vault. He'd make The Monroe a success, make his brother and family proud of him, prove to the world that he could do whatever the hell he set his mind to.

Having the music venue and playing occasionally would have to be enough to satisfy his creativity. Seeing Liam again hammered home how he'd crossed the point of no return.

CHAPTER 5

Kenzie double checked the tripod holding her smartphone and ring light. Satisfied she'd framed her yoga mat, the purple-tinged mountains, and the pink streaks of color lighting up the post-dawn sky, she set the camera's timer and hurried to sit cross-legged on her yoga mat. Time to film a Vinyasa yoga class for Yogadownload.com, the international website where she was a lead teacher.

She'd agreed with Jamie, Yogadownload's Boss Babe CEO, to film a few free classes at the resort. Win: win—great content for their website and free promotion for Sanctuary Spa.

The sparkling waters of the hotel pool, the skinny palms stretching toward the morning sky, and the light sand made a breathtaking back drop, sure to impart tranquility to students practicing at home. Plus, the thousands of online yoga students were potential resort guests.

The camera light flashed, and she sprang into teacher mode. "Good morning from beautiful Palm Springs. I'm Kenzie Banks and this is Sunrise Yoga Flow. And yes, I know it's a wee bit after sunrise, but we can pretend, right? Please find a comfortable seat on your mat and close your eyes. Let's take these first few minutes to turn your focus inward and filter out everything else. Start deepening your breath, taking full inhales and complete exhales. Let's––"

"Ahem, Kenzie?" A deep male voice called from much too close to her.

Her eyes snapped open, and there stood a half-naked Austin at the swimming pool's edge. All six foot something of him. He had a swimmer's frame: broad shoulders, square, chiseled pecs, ridged abs, narrow hips, and carved V-muscles descending into short black briefs. Not an ounce of extra flesh on his long, lean to-die-for body.

They'd both been busy with their respective jobs all week, and this was the first time she'd seen him up close since the other night. And…she was staring. Her mouth grew dry, and she cleared her throat.

"I'm filming. Or shall I say I was filming. Hold on." She scrambled to her feet, stalked to the camera, and stopped the video. Deleted the intro for good measure.

"Sorry about that. I was planning on getting in some laps before the workday started. I didn't notice the camera."

Her gaze sharpened on his face. His eyelids were heavy and faint bluish circles tinged the skin beneath his eyes. "Didn't get much sleep?"

"I'm not a great sleeper. Working out in the morning usually wakes me up." He blew out a breath and gestured toward the pool. "Hence the laps."

Keep it professional and fun. "And here I thought you'd changed your mind and wanted to practice yoga with me. I can get you a mat?"

"No thanks. I'm not flexible at all."

She rolled her eyes. "Like I said before, that's why you practice yoga––to get and stay flexible. I was filming a class for Yogadownload before the construction crew arrives, while it's still quiet around here." Or was quiet for a few blessed moments.

"Will me swimming laps distract you? And what's Yogadownload?"

"It's an online yoga website and app. You can stream classes from anywhere on your phone or computer or even your TV. I usually film in studio but wanted to do a few classes here--free advertising."

"Great idea. So should I wait until you're finished filming?"

"You aren't going to cannon ball into the pool and do the Butterfly stroke or anything, are you? I was going to film for 45 minutes."

He laughed. "Um, no. I'm not that aggressive. Nice quiet freestyle and maybe a little backstroke."

She kept her gaze on his square-jawed face and refused to allow her eyes to drop below his neck. Yeah, her peripheral vision worked too well. But she was a consummate professional.

She could film yoga with all kinds of external noise and distractions--heck, in India the sounds, sights, and smells never ceased, and she'd been able to meditate just fine. One extra-hot, wet, slippery rockstar within mere feet of her was amateur hour. Yeah, right.

She replied in her serene teaching voice, "That should be fine. I'm miked up which helps filter out external noises. How long will you be?"

He shrugged. "I usually just do thirty minutes when I'm crunched for time. Enough to quiet my mind and get the blood flowing."

Under no circumstances consider where his blood is flowing. "I can give you all that with yoga."

Watching him would certainly scramble her mind and

pump up her own blood flow. Her pulse had accelerated the moment she'd opened her eyes and seen him in front of her.

His lips twitched. "You're persistent. I promise I'll do some yoga with you in the mornings soon."

And it was probably safer that way. "I'm going to hold you to it. I'll wait until you're in the pool before I start the camera."

"Deal. And I'll be stealthy getting out." He dropped his towel, strolled to the edge of the pool, and dove in without even a trace of a splash.

Of course, he would be talented at that too. The guy was too good at just about everything he'd done since she'd met him. Well, with the exception of organization and punctuality. But she could handle it.

She took a cleansing breath and pressed play.

AUSTIN STROKED his way across the pool, praying the chilly water would cool him off. And, holy hell, the way her lavender sports bra and violet leggings emphasized her slim but curvy physique, the defined muscles of her shoulders and arms, and her long shapely legs. Raw desire surged through him. Her sexy body was now imprinted on his brain.

He picked up the pace—maybe the physical exertion would extinguish his hard-on since the cold water hadn't. So much for the shrinkage theory. It was only her first week and he'd already spilled his guts about Tommy and sported a woody in swim trunks.

He kicked faster and sliced his arms through the water like a white shark was tracking him. Through sheer willpower, he shut off his brain and tuned into his body. Sixty laps should do the trick.

After the last punishing length of the pool, he rested his

forearms on the cement border and worked to regulate his breathing. After about twenty laps, he'd calmed down.

Don't look. Don't look. Don't look. And, of course, he looked.

Now Kenzie knelt on her mat, with her hands resting on her heels, her chest pointing up to the sky, and her head dropped back, exposing her slender throat. And just like that, he was stone hard. Again.

Being out here with her was dangerous. Time to bolt back to his suite.

He pulled himself out of the water, padded over to grab his towel, and wrapped it around his waist to camouflage the situation in his shorts.

He glanced back to where Kenzie was now holding boat pose--his least favorite exercise from his days with the evil personal trainer who had toured with his band. Her smile was wide, like the pose was easy and didn't require a powerful core. Not so much.

He waved and strode toward his room. Time to shower and bury himself in work. Damn it, he'd probably need to take an extra-long shower because seeing Kenzie on her knees triggered all kinds of filthy fantasies. Like his fist wrapped in her long, silky hair while she knelt in front of him.

Avoidance should be simple enough. Today consisted of back to back meetings which would require his undivided attention. And according to Kenzie's detailed business plan, she'd have a full day, too.

Sometimes a hasty retreat was the wisest move.

CHAPTER 6

Kenzie forced her gaze to remain on the turquoise sky and not follow Austin's return to his room. With a frustrated exhale, she sprang to her feet and stopped the video. Darn it, she'd been teaching yoga for almost a decade and practicing since she was twelve years old. Her powers of concentration were generally excellent, yet she hadn't been able to filter out the visual of Austin's muscular frame in the water.

How long had she been teaching Yoga Sutra 1:2 *Chitta Vritti Nirodha,* which stated yoga is learning to direct your attention where you want it to go--essentially eliminating distractions and controlling your mind. Sounded simple but definitely not easy.

Around Austin Michaels? More like impossible. She snorted as she rolled up her yoga mat. Maybe she should stop pushing him to do private yoga with her, at least until she got her hormones under control. Something about him gave her tingles from head to toe--him bending and twisting and breathing deeply next to her would not be ideal. More like the opposite of ideal.

In her early twenties, she'd been the classic child of alcoholics––always looking to save the charismatic, reckless guys. The ones who had so much potential. Guys like her parents. Selfish people who drained her emotionally––always taking and never giving. Teaching yoga helped her set personal boundaries because she learned she could pour her nurturing energy into helping her students instead of trying to save men who didn't want to change.

Austin emanated easy charm and a hint of swagger. Even though he didn't seem selfish, his demons were just beneath the surface and part of her itched to try to help him. She'd sworn never to get involved with another bad boy with a tortured soul again.

Despite the palpable chemistry between them, he was trouble. Something about him tempted her to throw caution to the wind but neither of them could afford complications.

"Ugh." She marched back to her suite. If only she could quiet her overactive brain easily, the way she taught her students. But mastering the mind was a lifelong yogi goal and she was no master. Obviously.

When she entered her room, she crossed to the desk which faced the jagged mountains and checked today's schedule. Booked down to the minute, just how she loved it. Time to gather herself and resurrect her defenses around him. Friendly and professional––end of story.

Her phone rang, with a number she didn't recognize. "Hello, this is Kenzie."

"Kenzie, hi. It's Lucy Goodwin, Hotel Kings' wedding planner. Do you have a minute to chat?" a sweet voice asked.

"Hi Lucy, what can I do for you?"

"Well, two things, actually. First, I'd like to set up a Zoom call to discuss cross-promotion between Sanctuary Spa and the wedding venues here. You're planning on hosting bridal parties there, right?"

"Absolutely. I'm already drafting a special group spa menu. So, you're thinking of referring us business, right? How can I reciprocate?"

"Well, that's what I want to discuss. I can send you an email with some ideas, and we can meet once you've had a chance to review it and send me your feedback."

Kenzie grinned. "Austin said you were organized. I love it. That's how I work best."

"Oh good, I wasn't sure if you'd be more loosey-goosey like Austin."

"Really?" She frowned.

"Oh, I don't mean to offend you, I just figured since you teach yoga, you'd might not be as anal as I am." Lucy's voice was apologetic.

"Not offended at all. They don't call yoga a discipline for nothing. Flexible doesn't mean I'm not super organized. I'm on board."

Lucy snort laughed. "Between Charlie, you, and me, poor Austin doesn't stand a chance."

"Well, I can't wait to meet you in person and spend some time with Charlie outside of our initial interview. I'm always happy to meet kindred souls."

"On that note, I have a proposition for you. You're part of the team now and we'd really like to get to know you better."

Kenzie's heart warmed. "That's so sweet. Are you planning on coming out here? Isn't it peak wedding season right now?"

"No, we want you to come here. Well, first meet us in L.A. and then come out to Monterey at the end of the month."

"Oh, I'm not sure I can get away. I've got a really tight schedule with the Labor Day opening." Kind of odd Lucy didn't realize this.

"Hear me out. Charlie and Ryan are getting married at the end of the month here at Cypress Coast Ranch. She'd like for you to join us for the bachelorette party in L.A. a week from Saturday and then fly out to Monterey with Austin for the wedding."

Kenzie sucked in a breath. "Really? I don't want to intrude on a family get-together."

"Oh no, you wouldn't be. I don't know if you realized it when you signed on to become part of the management team, but we're family. Ryan and Austin are brothers, and the other guys were all ROTC together back in college. Campbell and Cameron are siblings and I've known them all since high school. So now, you're part of all of this."

Kenzie pressed a hand to her heart. "Wow, I don't know what to say." Lucy couldn't know she essentially didn't have her own family.

"Say yes. We've got a limo booked in West Hollywood, the same night the guys are going out in L.A. We'll get dressed up all fancy and go dancing. It will be a blast."

"Well, okay. Yes, I'll come. I understand the bachelorette party will be a great time to bond with everyone, but the wedding seems like too much? Again, I don't want to impose."

"Look, Charlie and Ryan, and me for that matter, wouldn't invite you to come unless we wanted you there. Okay? We're all pretty blunt in our own ways. And it will be a great way for you to really see everyone's dynamics in a casual environment."

"Well, I'd love that. Part of why I chose to come on board is that up until now, I've always opened and launched spas and then moved on. Now that I'm getting closer to 30, I want to plant roots. So, thank you."

"Excellent. I'll email you the bachelorette details. We've got a hotel suite for the night so just meet us there."

"Sounds good. And what about the wedding arrangements? Should I just come in for the day?"

"Oh no, you might remember that Monterey isn't the easiest place to get to, which is one of the reasons we love it. Chris, Ryan and Austin's stepdad, is splurging with a private plane. They were already planning on picking up Austin in Palm Springs on Friday and letting him use it to return on Sunday."

"Private plane?" Just who was his dad?

"Bougie, right? Chris McNeill, their stepdad, is a movie director and has connections. But he's so down to earth, you'd never know."

"Sure, that works." Now she'd be flying on private jets with her boss's parents? Talk about surreal.

"Great. I'll send you all the wedding details, too. It's going to be amazing. Oh, and just so you know, I've got you sitting with Austin at the bridal party table."

"You what?" Nerves danced down her spine.

"It's no big deal. All the guys are in the wedding party, so the bridal party is basically the management team."

"Doesn't he have a date for his brother's wedding?" Simply curiosity, right? *Right.*

"No. Then I figured it would not only be efficient for you to sit with us, but it's a little selfish."

"Selfish?" Efficient was one way of putting it. Really frickin' awkward was another. But selfish?

"Well, now the reception photos will look better. It's a buffet but the wedding party table is up on a dais. If Austin had come solo, it would look unbalanced. It warms my little heart." Lucy laughed.

Kenzie chuckled. What else could she do? "Glad I can help make the reception photos symmetrical. I'm looking forward to meeting you and hanging out next week. I've got to run and get ready for a meeting."

"Perfect. You're a lifesaver. I'll email you the details now. Thanks so much. Talk later."

The phone went dark and for a moment she stared at the blank screen. Three things were true.

One: Her meditations had been focused on manifesting a real home so, Lucy's invitation was a step in that direction.

Two: With all the time she'd be spending with Austin on a personal level, she would have to work hard to maintain her distance. They'd be traveling together, sitting with each other, how was she going to be able to avoid him? She wasn't. Their physical attraction was undeniable, and she feared the more she got to know him, the more his sheer presence would impact her emotions, too.

Three: Time to tap into every single mindfulness technique at her disposal to level out her emotions. Including getting on with her busy day.

Before she could pull up her schedule, her phone rang again. Another number she didn't recognize, but she had so many balls in the air right now and so many interviews and meetings, screening wasn't an option.

"Hello, this is Kenzie Banks."

"Oh, hello Ms. Banks, this is Melissa Maclean, the massage therapist. I was calling to check where to go for my massage audition today at 4:30?"

Kenzie hurried over to her paper planner and flipped to today's schedule. "Of course. Yes, I've got space set up in the spa for you and Carly for partner massages."

"Oh great, Carly and I are friends and we're both so excited for the resort to open."

"Me too. I'll see you this afternoon. You'll both bring massage tables and all supplies, correct?"

The spa building was full of boxes containing everything from oils to massage tables and towels. It would all have to be unpacked and set up but not until the building was fully remodeled.

"Oh yes, of course. Do you need us to bring everything?"

"Yes please. The spa renovation isn't finished yet." And having rough surroundings would also help show how professional the two therapists were. Being flexible and making the massage soothing regardless of external setting was vital.

"Absolutely. I'm looking forward to meeting you in person, Ms. Banks. Thank you so much."

"Me too. And please excuse all the construction. Just drive around and park by the spa building. You know where it is?"

"I do. I remember the old hotel before it closed down. My mom worked there, and I used to come by when I was a little girl. We're all so happy you're bringing it back to life."

"Oh, that's lovely. I've got to run now but I'll see you this afternoon, Melissa."

Kenzie sank into her office chair. And realized she didn't have another body for Carly's audition.

Austin's lean muscled frame popped into her brain. Again. He'd mentioned his stress and insomnia. Obviously, he was working hard and needed to relax. But could she really lay on a massage table next to him, practically naked, while they were both rubbed and stroked?

She shook her head. Would she have asked her manager at any other resort? Of course she would. And Austin did say he enjoyed massages. She swiveled in the chair and scanned the stark horizon. Not even a whisper of a cloud broke up the miles of blue sky.

She tapped her fingers against her lips. What would be the best way to ask--no, she wasn't asking--the best way to tell Austin he was getting a massage with her this afternoon?

Should she text him or call him? Right now, she didn't want to face him, not after this morning. No, she needed some space today to regain her professional footing.

She snorted. Yeah, like getting massages a few feet apart was the height of discretion and professionalism. She'd just text him to meet her at the spa for a few final interviews. Yeah, that worked. She needed his input.

Time to cement their relationship as friendly colleagues.

Simple but not easy.

CHAPTER 7

"Hello?" Austin stepped into the cavernous spa building. Stacked boxes leaned against the unpainted walls. Tarps covered the floors of the spacious lobby awaiting fancy marble tiles.

"We're back here, in the treatment area." Kenzie's voice echoed from the wide high-ceilinged hallway to the left of the entrance.

He followed her voice, noting how the building's thick walls kept the space cool. When she'd called last minute for his assistance with final interviews, he'd welcomed the interruption from his computer screen. Staffing had been one of his favorite parts of his role managing the bar in New York––people over paperwork anytime.

When he reached the open doorway, he halted in his tracks. Two massage tables stood side by side. Kenzie awaited him with two smiling women.

"There you are." Kenzie's grin was unnaturally wide. "Melissa and Carly are ready for us."

"Hello ladies, I'm Austin, the GM. Are we doing the interviews here?" Odd.

"Oh, I've already interviewed them. Melissa's mom worked at the old hotel, isn't that cool? We're all set up for partner massages, which is the final portion of the hiring process."

Kenzie's cadence was usually smooth and controlled--now she was practically babbling. His eyes widened. "Partner massages?"

She swept her arm toward the tables. "Yes, it's when a couple or two friends have their massages at the same time, next to each other. It's very popular. You've never had one?"

He bit the inside of his cheek, enjoying her nervousness. "I have not, but I can see the appeal. I was just surprised, that's all." *Because you didn't mention anything about massages, particularly side by side. Huh.*

"Oh, I'm sorry if I didn't make it clear. It's the most effi-cient way to assess both therapists' techniques. Okay?" Her gaze was focused over his left shoulder.

He shrugged. Damn, he'd just promised himself to keep his distance and lying next to her naked body would test his limits.

The tall brunette spoke up. "We'll just step out so you can get changed. Please pick your table, lay face down, and call out when you're ready."

They exited through the open doorway.

"And where would you propose we change?" It wasn't like there was a divider set up.

Kenzie's cheeks pinkened. "Umm, how about we turn around and remove our clothes--there's a basket under each massage table--and slide under the sheets?"

Every muscle in his body stiffened. "Sure."

Neither one of them moved. The air thickened.

"How about on the count of three?"

He chuckled. "Sure. Three. Two. One."

He spun around and whipped off his t-shirt. Offered

thanks to the universe that he hadn't gone commando today. Was Kenzie in lace? A thong? All the blood in his body rushed to his dick.

"Tell me when it's safe to turnaround." Because if he caught a glimpse of her panties, he was royally screwed.

"I'm down. Your turn." Her voice was throaty, sexy. Tempting.

He dove onto the table, tugging the soft sheet up to his shoulders before turning his head toward her. *Be professional. Pretend this is just an interview.*

Kenzie had pulled her long golden hair into one of those messy buns. Her cheek rested on her stacked elbows. Sheer willpower enabled him to keep his gaze on her glowing face and not check out her silhouette under the thin sheet covering her.

"Okay, this table is really comfortable. One of ours?" His voice sounded relatively normal, not like he was lying on a steel kickstand.

"No, ours are still in boxes, with almost all the equipment. I'm waiting until the renovations are complete before tackling all the unpacking. Carly and Melissa brought their own." Kenzie's serene voice had returned.

"Well, I'd say that's a point in their favor because I've had some crappy tables in my day and this one is great." What was he blathering about? Was he the only one losing it?

"Agreed. If their hands live up to their resumes, I say we hire them."

"Sounds good to me." If he survived.

He was being professional, right? All he had to do was stay face down on the table. Not think about being close enough to reach over and stroke one hand along her silky shoulder.

She called out Melissa's name and the women returned.

"Great, you two are ready to go. I brought a speaker and some music, is that okay with you?" Carly said.

"Of course. And we'll just go for 45 minutes, okay? Deep tissue/Swedish."

Melissa smiled down at him. "Okay, anything going on I should know about? Any areas of your body bothering you?"

Well, my dick will leave a permanent indentation in your massage table... "My lower back is a little tight. I like firm pressure."

"Excellent. I'll check in as we proceed, and you just tell me if you want me to back off or go deeper. Is unscented lotion okay or do you prefer oil?"

He stifled a groan. Now he had a visual of Kenzie's pale skin slicked up with oil. "Lotion, please."

"I'd love the lavender oil, Carly. And I like it deep. Don't be afraid to work and use firm pressure."

Austin fingers curled into fists. Yeah, the next 45 minutes were going to test his endurance for torture. *Fuck, fuck, fuck. Do not under any circumstances visualize Kenzie telling you to go deeper and stronger.*

"Mmm, just like that. It feels so good," Kenzie moaned.

"Can you relax your hands, Austin? Your muscles feel like steel cords. Just take a few deep breaths," Melissa murmured.

He consciously forced his muscles to slacken. But his frickin' hard-on wasn't softening anytime soon. Deep breaths, he'd take deep breaths.

Mercifully, Kenzie quieted down and the soothing music mix finally filtered into his brain. Melissa went full deep tissue on him, and the borderline painful pressure succeeded in redirecting his attention. Better to focus on the knots in his lower back--safer anyway.

By the time the treatment ended, and the therapists stepped out of the room, he'd regained control over his body. When he sat up, he dared to glance at Kenzie. Her cheeks were flushed, her red-gold hair was a mess, and she had black rings beneath her eyes from her smudged mascara. She looked like she'd just been thoroughly fucked.

And so was he. So much for self-control.

And this was their first week working together.

Now he'd heard the sounds she made when she enjoyed the way someone touched her. And he'd seen what she'd look like if it had been his hands giving her pleasure. Imagined if he'd used his mouth. Dreamed of being buried deep inside her.

Kenzie flashed a Cheshire cat grin. "Well, I don't know about Melissa, but Carly was amazing. She's hired as far as I'm concerned. What do you think?"

"I'm sold on Melissa. She was excellent. If you've checked their references and completed the interviews, I approve."

"Great. And thanks for being a guinea pig. We'll have more therapists coming through, so get ready to be pampered."

He hopped off the table, careful to wrap the sheet around him. "I'll have to see."

"Come on, free massages are one of the best perks of hiring. Don't you feel better?"

Better wasn't exactly what he'd call it. More like primed and ready to go. "I'm actually too relaxed. I need to wake up. I'm going to take a swim and tackle some more paperwork. See you later." Time to cool off. Again.

"Okay. I'd scheduled in a swim too. Do you mind?"

"It's your pool too. See ya later." Like he could refuse without exposing his over the top reaction to her proximity. Avoiding her gaze, he marched toward his suite.

AUSTIN THREW on some board shorts and thanked the universe nothing urgent was pending, at least for the next half an hour. A quick swim would cool him down. Then he'd be able to compartmentalize his attraction to Kenzie and focus on the mountain of work waiting on his desk. That was the plan anyway.

Something about Mackenzie Banks pulled at him. Not just her objective beauty, but the combination of strength and sweetness she radiated. The woman would take no bull-shit, but she'd be kind about it.

He crossed the stone pathway to the pool and his step hitched. Kenzie had beaten him and sliced through the water with a smooth freestyle. Her bathing suit clad body was mostly submerged. Thank god.

He tossed his towel, and dove in. When he reached the deep end, he paused and turned, treading water. Kenzie rose from the shallow end like Aphrodite from the sea.

"Hey there. This pool is the best, right?" She wore a red and white polka-dot one-piece that shouldn't have been sexy--the neckline wasn't even low-cut. But her sculpted shoulders and arms, and her delicate collarbone beckoned for his touch. And he was losing his ever-loving mind.

"Yeah, it sure is." So much for what his buddies called his "quicksilver wit."

"I'm just going to swim a few more laps." A few beats later, Kenzie took off again.

He shoved his hair back from his face and reminded himself why he was in the pool--to swim.

For the next twenty minutes or so, they settled into a rhythm and his system settled. Probably because he couldn't hear or see her. Finally, he stopped at the shallow end and reclined back onto the highest step, letting his heartrate decrease.

She joined him, out of breath. "Okay, I can't believe I'm so out of shape. Those laps wiped me out."

"Nah, you know how it is when you do something for the first time in a while. You seem pretty fit to me." Out of shape? Compared to an Olympian?

She smiled and smoothed her hair back from her face. "Yoga and exercise are how I manage stress. Swimming definitely isn't my strongest talent. But I think living here, I'm going to be in the pool a lot more."

"During the hotter months, for sure, unless you're in the gym. Okay, I've got to get back to work."

"Me too." She ascended the pool steps just as he stood and turned.

She stumbled, her long fingers curling around his biceps. He caught her slender waist, steadying her.

She sucked in a sharp inhale, her pink lips parted.

"Kenzie." His gaze dropped to her tempting mouth.

She lifted her gaze, her ocean blue eyes almost black. She swayed, her grip tightening on his arms. "Austin, I--"

Heat flooded his system. *Danger.* He released her and scrambled out of the pool. "You okay?"

"Sorry about that. I'm not usually so clumsy." She gave a shaky laugh.

Her nipples were tight peaks, visible through the fabric of her suit. The sooner he retreated, the better. Her proximity was dangerous.

He grabbed his towel. "Don't worry about it. Okay, have a good rest of your night."

And with that, he bolted, intent on getting as far away from her as possible. Because he had been a split second away from kissing her. He slammed the door of his suite behind him. Locked it for good measure.

How would she taste, how would her tight, toned body

feel plastered against his, how would her tongue feel swirling with his?

Would she make that humming noise in the back of her throat when he slanted his mouth across hers? Would all the skin on her delectable body be as silky as it looked?

So much for the pool cooling him off.

He strode to the bathroom and flipped on the shower, turned it all the way to freezing. Yeah, time for another ice cold shower and a solo session with his right hand.

One fact was crystal clear--he needed to avoid her unless it was of vital importance to hotel business. Because if today were any indication, his attraction to her was risky. No shame in hiding. No choice but evasion if he were going to prove to the rest of the guys and his family that he could be a responsible grown-up and manage this hotel.

No choice at all.

CHAPTER 8

Kenzie ran her fingernail along the neatly written afternoon agenda in her tangerine and aqua striped paper planner. She compared it to the spreadsheet on her laptop and grimaced--she only had thirty minutes to grab a salad from the gourmet grocery store down the street. All week, she'd overscheduled herself in a futile attempt to stop obsessing over what she loosely referred to as the "pool incident."

Austin's streamlined swimmer's body. The scrape of his strong calloused hands on her wet skin when she'd stumbled on the pool steps. The flash of his grin and his way with words. The hint of the forbidden simmering beneath his casual guy façade.

Overall, she'd been able to compartmentalize. Well, except at night once she'd turned off the lights to go to sleep. That's when the fantasies of threading her fingers through Austin's shaggy dark hair and pulling his chiseled face in for a kiss heated her blood. And here she was, disappointed he hadn't kissed her.

"Enough." She huffed out a breath, grabbed her purse and

rushed outside. If she was going to be on time for a Zoom call to negotiate a deal with one of her favorite yoga suppliers for the spa's yoga studio, she needed to hurry.

When she unlocked her white convertible VW bug--not that she'd dare put the lid down and risk frying like an egg-- a wave of oppressive heat slammed into her. A few moments later, she deemed it safe to get in. The moment she flicked on the engine, her phone rang with the *Jaws* theme ringtone.

Her mood deflated like a punctured tire--her mother. She debated ignoring it, but the woman wouldn't stop until she'd reached her. May as well get it over with. She activated the Bluetooth and her mom's voice filled the small vehicle.

"Hello, Mother." She attempted to keep her voice light.

"Mackenzie? Is that you?"

Kenzie swallowed a snort of disbelief. Who else would it be? "It sure is. What can I do for you?"

"Can't your mother just call you to chat? I haven't heard from you in so long, I wanted to make sure my only daughter was okay." Patricia Banks' voice wavered.

Her mother didn't have any friends because she couldn't be bothered to express interest or listen to what anybody else said unless it was about her. It was exhausting.

"I let you know I started my new job and it's always hectic for the months leading up to opening day. I'm just very busy."

Her mother heaved out a melodramatic sigh. "I don't know what I did to you for you to ignore me this way. I was talking to the nurse practitioner at my doctor's office, and she said her children call her at least three times a week."

Maybe the nurse practitioner had actually loved her children? "Is everything okay? Why were you at the doctor's office?"

"You don't remember anything I tell you." Another noisy sigh. "My arthritis has been acting up again. I think I need to have to have my other knee replaced. It's so painful--you have no compassion. And I'm having terrible stomach pains and my head hurts constantly. It's probably a brain tumor."

And the hypochondria continued. "It's not a brain tumor. You're sure your doctors have cross-checked your medications? You know that they can have terrible side-effects when you mix them. If you could try to wean off--"

"Oh please. You have no idea what it feels like to be me. Your frou-frou green juices and witch doctor potions can't help me. The next thing you'll probably try to push on me is that marijuana stuff." And there she was--the venomous Patricia Banks.

Kenzie counted to three before responding. "CBD is extremely helpful for managing pain. As are alternative and holistic therapies. Even cutting out the processed foods and sugars make a big difference. Are you still drinking soda?"

"Anyway, I drink diet soda. It has no calories or no sugar. You're so judgmental. You didn't get that from me. You must have gotten that from your father, who is no help at all. I barely eat anything, and I can't lose weight. I have a tiny slice of grapefruit in the morning, really just a sliver and--" Her whine reached a high-pitched decibel only dogs could discern.

"Mother, I'm sure you didn't call me to tell me about what you eat every day. I don't mean to cut you off, but I've got an appointment in a few minutes I need to prepare for." Although her appetite had evaporated, and her stomach was in knots.

Her mother huffed out a breath. "I don't know what I did to deserve such an unloving daughter. Do you know the sacrifices I made for you? My figure was never the same after I had you and--"

So now her birth almost thirty years ago was still the cause of her mother's yo-yo dieting. "Got to go. Take care."

Kenzie hung up and powered off the phone for good

measure. She dropped her head onto the steering wheel, squealed, and jerked back. The thing was boiling hot. Sure enough, when she peeked in the rearview mirror, a red streak branded her forehead. She closed her eyes and blew out a breath.

Over the years, she'd lounged on many a therapist's couch learning how to create healthy boundaries. None had existed with her parents. In her early romantic relationships, she'd bent over backwards for the narcissistic careless men she'd chosen. All of them with some type of addiction problem to boot. Talk about patterns.

Step by step. She'd drive to the store, get a juice and salad. Maybe even indulge in some of the gourmet dark chocolate truffles they sold. Although right now, she felt like curling up in a ball on her bed with the drapes drawn.

Talking to that woman for even a few minutes threw her for a loop every time. The guilt, the tone of voice, the sheer selfishness. Maybe one day she'd make it through a call with her mother without her stomach twisting into ropes, but not today.

Had the woman ever once praised her for her accomplishments? Heck, her mother had almost missed her high school graduation ceremony and had skipped her college graduation because she'd had a "headache."

More like a hangover from an all-night drinking binge with her father. Not that he bothered to attend any events either. She could count on one hand, okay maybe two, the times he'd ever appeared in public sober. The humiliation of having him rant and rave and tell ridiculous stories never diminished. Better for him not to show up.

Reset time. She fired up the engine and flipped on a mellow piano radio station. Soothing music and a little yoga philosophy were in order. Time to implement one of her favorite Yoga Sutras or threads of wisdom, Yoga sutra

2.33 (*Vitarka-badhane   pratipaksha-bhavanam*):   When disturbed by negative thoughts, cultivate the opposite mental attitude.

In other words, when the negative thought or emotion pops up, immediately replace it with the positive. And... repeat. It worked really well to focus on gratitude and not get mired down in negativity.

So now, she had stopped falling for bad boys, she had finally found a resort where she could not only create the perfect spa but where she could stay and run it, and she was building a good life. Crappy parents wouldn't define the rest of her life. The desire to be the complete opposite of her parents truly defined her. Growing up with a narcissistic victim alcoholic mom and a reckless absentee dad would do that for you.

Anyway. She buzzed over to the grocery store and grabbed her favorite salmon and avocado salad. No way would she allow her mom's phone call to derail her day, like she'd done when she was younger.

She snagged a parking spot beneath an enormous palm tree which offered a sliver of shade in The Monroe lot. Just as she was crossing the stone walkway to the glamorous grand entrance, a flicker of awareness caused her to look up. There stood a grinning Austin with a tall ginger haired man and a lanky brunette. He waved her over.

Maybe her heartrate kicked up a notch. Maybe her mouth grew dry. Probably just the heat. Nothing to do with Mr. Tall, Dark, and Dangerous.

Cue her internal eyeroll. At least they wouldn't be alone the first time they talked since the "pool incident." Her chemical reaction to Austin threatened all she was working to accomplish.

Grateful for her dark sunglasses, she approached the trio. "Hi there."

Her meeting started in ten minutes, so she had an excuse not to linger.

"Hi Kenzie, these are my parents, Chris and Angela McNeill. Mom and Chris, this is Kenzie Banks, our Spa Manager."

"Nice to meet you." She smiled at the couple.

"Lovely to meet you, Kenzie. We've heard great things about you and the spas you create," Angela said.

"Thank you so much." Her gaze flicked toward Austin. "I'm hoping Sanctuary Spa will be an international draw for the resort. Are you two here for a visit?"

"We're checking out a location for a movie and stopped in for a quick hello with our youngest," Chris said in a deep baritone. "You should join us for dinner tonight if you're not busy. We'd love to hear more about how everything is progressing."

"Oh, that's so kind of you. I wouldn't want to intrude on a family dinner."

"Don't be silly. The more the merrier. And we're sharing the plane to Monterey in a few weeks, right?" Angela's voice was warm.

"They just want to pump you for information about the renovations. He's an investor in the hotels and sometimes I'm not the most… detail-oriented person." Austin cleared his throat.

She pressed a hand to her chest. Was that a hint of vulnerability in his voice? "I appreciate the invitation, but I've got back to back meetings through the evening. But I'm sure Austin can fill you in. Everything's going well so far."

Austin smirked. "Yeah, she's a planner, like Lucy and Charlie."

"You've got your special gifts, sweetie, and you're lucky to have all the organized women around you." His mom wrapped an arm around him and ruffled his dark hair.

A stab of envy pierced her heart. It was apparent Austin was close to his parents and they adored him. What would that be like? To have parents who went out of their way to visit and spend time with their children? Who accepted them just as they were? Angela and her own mother couldn't be more different.

And on that note, she needed to retreat. "I do need to run but it was lovely to meet you both and I'll see you all later."

Meeting Austin's mom and stepdad raised more questions about his past. Was his biological father not in the picture?

Well, the next few weeks she'd have a front row seat to everyone's personal dynamics. As long as she could avoid questions about her own background, she'd be golden. Nobody needed to know her sad, dysfunctional little story.

She'd buried those demons and reinvented herself. So why did her heart ache?

CHAPTER 9

*K*enzie drummed her fingers on the steering wheel to David Bowie's *Modern Love,* an appropriate 80s tune for the drive to Charlie's bachelorette party. Not that she could carry a note--singing was most definitely not one of her strengths. But alone in her car, she could screech to her heart's content, as long as she kept the windows closed. No need to summon the rattlesnakes and coyotes.

The upbeat music carried her along Highway 10 past the windmill fields and expanses of barren desert. Now the high-rises of downtown Los Angeles loomed against a hazy horizon. She hadn't spent much time in the City of Angels, and certainly not clubbing with coworkers and strangers.

She swallowed the nerves bubbling up in her throat. She was good in groups and was looking forward to making some personal connections. Or so she kept telling herself.

She exited on North Highland toward Sunset Boulevard and followed the GPS directions to the Pendry West Holly-wood Hotel. Lucy had booked the penthouse suite for the night. She'd offered to be the evening's designated driver, but

Lucy had laughed her off, explaining they had a limo for the night. Nothing to be done but have a blast.

Fine by her. Although hopefully it wouldn't make anyone uncomfortable that she didn't drink. Sometimes people tried to encourage her to "have just one" or questioned her about why she abstained. Somehow she figured nobody wanted an honest answer of "oh my parents are raging alcoholics and my childhood was horrific."

She pulled up to the mid-century modern building with broad expanses of glass and sleek lines. The valet informed her that unfortunately the hotel lot was at capacity, but she could use the lot next door for overflow parking. Not a problem for her.

When she reached the gorgeous lobby, she paused to admire the black and white marble floors, deep azure walls, and velvet furnishings. Although the décor was modern, it radiated warmth and welcome. And it was pretty darn fancy--she liked how these women rolled.

Because the rest of the group had arrived earlier and spent the afternoon by the pool, Lucy had texted her the suite number. She bypassed reception and ascended to the top floor. A frisson of anxiety sparked through her, and she paused in front of the door. These women wanted her here, right? They had insisted she come, so she'd go with it. She drew up to her full height and knocked.

A petite redhead with dark doe eyes whipped open the door and frowned. "Hey there, you're not room service."

Kenzie did a double take when an identical redhead swatted the woman's shoulder. "Hi, I'm Dylan and this is my rude sister, Sam. You're Mackenzie, right?" She smiled apologetically.

Aha--Austin's twin stepsisters. "Call me Kenzie, please. Nice to meet you."

Sam yanked the door open wider. "Sorry about that,

Kenzie, I'm starving and hoped you were my large pizza. Come on in."

Dylan waved an arm toward the suite. "We're so glad you could make it. Come meet everyone."

"Thanks so much." Kenzie smiled. If the rest of the crew were as casual as these two, the evening would be just fine.

She followed the McNeill twins through a high-ceilinged foyer with aquamarine walls and polished hardwood floors. It opened into an enormous living area where the afternoon sunlight sparkled through tall vertical windows highlighting the gleaming wood and blue velvet furniture. A gaggle of gorgeous women lounged on the couches, sipping champagne and nibbling veggies.

Charlie hurried over in a blur of long tawny limbs and honey blonde hair and clasped both of her hands. "Kenzie, you made it. Thanks so much for coming."

"Thanks for inviting me."

"Well, first things first. This weekend, I am not remotely your boss, just your new friend. Second, let me introduce you to everyone." Charlie released one hand and pointed at Snow White's doppelganger. "That's Olivia, she's a librarian currently living in Greece and Grant's significant other."

The stunning brunette waved. "Welcome."

"You already met Dylan and Sam. That's Amanda, their older sister who is the equine vet at Pacific Coast Ranch, where the McNeills and the Michaels brothers grew up."

The delicate blonde with jade-colored eyes smiled, "It's nice to meet you."

"The other ginger is Phoebe, Amanda's sister in law. That's Campbell, our master sommelier who is engaged to Jack, and they live in Paso Robles and work at Maison du Soleil. Camille is her sister. You've spoken to Lucy, our fabulous wedding planner who is engaged to Cameron, who runs our Monterey property. Jenny is Sam's sister in law, and that gorgeous brunette on the end is my best friend Brigitte."

"There will be a quiz later, so I hope you paid attention." Brigitte lilted in a French accent.

"Please, no quiz. Hi everyone, I can't wait to hang out with you all." Kenzie prided herself on remembering names––it came with the territory of teaching group yoga classes, but it might take a hot minute to keep all these women straight.

Campbell waved an elegant hand. "No tests at the party. Just fun. Can I get you some bubbles? I brought an excellent French brut rosé."

Kenzie shook her head. "I'd actually love some water with bubbles if you've got some?"

Lucy rose from the couch and headed toward a long buffet table filled with bottles. "I'm feeling like some sparkling water too. We even have limes and grapefruit slices."

"I'd love lime. And wow, this place is amazing. Is this going to be competition for the Beverly Hills location?"

Brigitte tucked a strand of dark hair behind her ear. "It shouldn't be. I'll be moving here to be the concierge at the Beverly Hills hotel and based on my research, Beverly Hills and West Hollywood attract two different sets of clientele."

Lucy handed her a crystal glass and clapped her hands together. "Okay ladies, here's the plan. The limo is picking us up in two hours so it's time to shower and get ready. And I've got a few surprises before we leave. Deal?"

Charlie wagged a finger at Lucy. "There absolutely will not be any penis necklaces or straws or any other penis-type paraphernalia. Understood?"

"Oh come on, Charlie. Not even a penis barrette? Ryan would love it." Sam threw back her head and laughed.

Charlie's lips twitched. "Yeah right. Your brother would

love that since he isn't uptight at all. Don't even think about it."

Brigitte laughed. "Don't worry ma chérie, I will protect you. But you *will* wear a tiara because I brought one for each of us from the Turks and Caicos. They are sparkly and elegant and will make you look like the wedding queen you will be."

"Fine. But only if everyone wears them." Charlie scanned the room with narrowed eyes. "Okay, I'm going to take a shower." She pivoted and disappeared through one of the doorways.

"Tiaras will be perfect." Lucy beamed. "Okay Kenzie, follow me. We're sharing a room."

Kenzie picked up her bag and did as she was told. "I showered before I left so I just need to do hair and makeup."

"I like your style. Let's go get fancy."

THE GROUP of women in small sparkly dresses and large shiny tiaras tumbled into the white stretch limousine after stop number three. Everyone but Kenzie had been slamming tequila shots and guzzling skinny margaritas, but despite the heavy drinking, she felt comfortable.

What a gathering of strong, take-no-bullshit women—from Sam being one of the top horse breeding managers in the country to Campbell being one of the world's handful of master sommeliers—they all had impressive careers. But beyond their professional accomplishments, they were down to earth. The night had been filled with laughter and genuine affection. And they made her feel welcome, like she'd been one of the pack all along.

No way could they suspect just how much belonging to a bonded group would mean to her. She didn't know how she'd gotten so lucky as to be part of it, but she hoped these relationships would develop into real lasting friendships. Like she'd always dreamed.

She glanced up and Charlie was huddled in the corner whispering into her phone, her hand hiding her face.

"Charlie--you better not be on a work call on your bachelorette party evening." Dylan pointed at her with one scarlet tipped fingernail.

Charlie quickly ended the call. She raised one hand, like she was being called on in school. "I have an announcement." She giggled.

Brigitte rolled her enormous eyes. "Uh-oh. If Charlie's giggling like a teenager, she's up to something. What did you do?"

Charlie glanced around the limo with a sheepish smile. "Now, this is my bachelorette party, right?" Her words held a slight slur.

Her question was met with a chorus of yeses.

She pressed her palm against her dress's gold sequin halter top. "So, you guys have to do what I say, right?"

This time the responses were a chorus of affirmative and maybes.

"Well, that was Ryan, and we want to meet up at the Kitty Kat Klub to go dancing. Austin got us on the VIP list so we can stroll right in have a table with bottle service."

And just like that, the limo erupted.

"What? I thought we said no boys! Holt is with him, and I wanted him to miss me tonight." Sam pouted.

Olivia smirked. "Seriously? Can't you two spend one night apart? You can dance with him for the rest of your life."

"We should vote. Don't we get a say? Aren't we throwing you the party?" A crease appeared between Phoebe's ginger brows.

Lucy brought her fingers to her lips and whistled,

instantly silencing the cacophony. "It is Charlie's party and if she wants us to meet up with the guys, that's her prerogative. And Ryan even found a place named for our own crazy cat lady. So that's what we're going to do."

"And don't act like you don't want your guys seeing you all glammed up and looking so hot." Charlie wagged a finger at everyone.

Kenzie's breath caught in her throat. Almost all these women were paired up with their boyfriends, fiancés, or husbands. Which meant once they arrived at the Kitty Kat Klub—and what kind of name was that? --things could become awkward between her and Austin.

No need to panic. She released an extended exhale and allowed her eyes to close for a moment. She inhaled for a count of four and exhaled for a count of four, forcing the galloping of her heart to regulate. It would be *fine*.

He'd have women falling all over him and she'd be sitting there like the fifth wheel--or in the group's case, the twentieth wheel. He was a famous rockstar, well, famous ex-rockstar and at age thirty had only had one serious girlfriend.

Yeah, so maybe she'd googled him after that first day at the hotel. His ex was some supermodel who'd dumped him after she realized he wouldn't be lead singer of Black Velvet Machine again. Or so the tabloids claimed. Had she broken Austin's heart?

She dug her fingernails into her legs. She loved to dance, and it wasn't like she couldn't go off and find some hottie to dance with when everyone else coupled up. She was a big girl and was used to being on her own. And who knew? Maybe they'd all dance in a group.

Who could blame the buzzed, happy women for being excited to see their loves? She glanced at her watch. Maybe nobody would notice if she asked the limo driver to drop her back at the hotel? She'd planned on leaving early in the morning because she had tons of work to do tomorrow.

Maybe she could beg off with that excuse and avoid the whole scenario. Avoid Austin.

A hand squeezed her forearm, jolting her out of her escape plan. "I can see your mind whirring. Everything okay? This place is supposed to have some of the best DJs around so it should be a blast." Lucy's full lips curved upward.

Something about Lucy's sweetness tugged at her. "I just need to get on the road early tomorrow morning. You know how it is with prepping for the hotel opening."

No need for Lucy to suspect Kenzie had a secret crush on her boss or that she was nervous to see him. No need for anyone to know.

Lucy patted her arm. "Don't worry, it's still early. And you're not drinking so a hangover won't be an issue, unlike what the rest of this crew is facing tomorrow. And it is California so last call is at 1:30."

"Okay, okay, I'll go. If I decide to return to the hotel early, I'll let you know, don't worry."

"Of course. You're having fun though, right?" Lucy's wide chocolate brown eyes shone with concern.

"I am. You're great. Everyone is great." It was true. And she had a feeling these women were going to play an important part of her life going forward.

Tonight was fun.

Well, it had been fun until she'd learned she'd be seeing Austin at a bar.

The limo purred to a stop.

"We're here. Woo-hoo, this place won't know what hit it once we arrive. And Jack's jaw is going to drop to the floor when he sees me in this dress." Campbell shimmied her toned shoulders and snapped her fingers.

The chauffer opened the door, and they clambered out onto the sidewalk in a flurry of stilettos and giddy laughter.

A long line snaked around the corner of the industrial looking building, three people deep. Oh yeah, they weren't going to be thrilled when a dozen women sashayed right past them. Olivia and Lucy each linked an arm through hers and together they sauntered up to the ginormous mountain of a bouncer.

Charlie reached the guy first and by the time they caught up, the massive man had already unhooked the red rope and was gesturing toward the ornately carved emerald green door. Another giant ushered them inside, muttered something into the walkie-talkie pinned to his black jacket, and ordered them to follow him.

As if anybody would turn down the guy who looked like a cross between the Incredible Hulk and Goliath. They trailed single file behind him down a dim, narrow hallway, like some distorted version of a mama hen herding her chicks. Their chattering had ceased, as if they'd be scolded if they clucked too much. Kenzie giggled and bit her lip when the silly visual popped into her mind.

Thumping bass music reverberated through every cell of her body, like she was back in a European disco where the techno pop blasted non-stop. Not her favorite but it made it easy to dance all night since the songs bled one into the other. Flashing lights appeared as they approached the doorway into the main section of the nightclub.

Kenzie blinked and scanned the room. It was like an old school discotheque, complete with mirrored balls suspended from the high ceiling, an enormous dance floor, and booths framing the perimeter. The elevated seating allowed the occupants to survey the mass of writhing bodies pulsating to the powerful bass beat.

"There's Gabriel and the boys." Dylan pointed toward the

far corner of the room, where a group of guys waved at them.

All of the women except for her and Brigitte had found the loves of their lives and perhaps the green monster nipped her. She shook it off. Not her time. Once The Monroe opened and her spa was running smoothly, she'd start dating. Priorities.

As they approached the booth, Kenzie struggled not to gawk like a teenager at a Harry Styles concert. The gods had been smiling down when they created this selection of men, wow.

Ryan and Charlie were already kissing, plastered together against a tall column next to the booth, oblivious to everyone around them. One by one, the couples reunited, in a flurry of kisses. Kenzie's gut clenched and she retreated a step, intent on returning to the hotel. She pivoted toward the door.

Before she could flee, a warm hand landed on her bare shoulder and a shot of awareness shimmered down to her toes. Austin's clean masculine scent filled her nostrils and the heat from his lean muscular frame ratcheted up the temperature in the crowded nightclub.

She turned and even in her four-inch strappy heels, he had several inches on her. His tousled hair gleamed like onyx under the overhead lights, the shadows bouncing off his chiseled features.

His grinned and if she wasn't mistaken, it had a feral hint. "Can you believe these two? My big brother barely cracked a smile all night until he and Charlie started texting."

Heat bloomed low in her belly. She shifted away. "I think it's sweet."

He threw his head back and laughed. "Sweet isn't really a word I'd attribute to either of them, but they are crazy for each other. Can I get you a drink? We've got bottles at the table."

"Nothing to drink for me. Thanks."

His brows drew together. "I ordered some sparkling water once I learned you ladies were joining us. Nothing for you?"

"That was considerate of you. Thanks, that would be great." Her heart warmed--he remembered she didn't drink alcohol.

His hand moved to her lower back, and he gently guided her toward the booth. Every single nerve ending in her body screamed danger, danger. At least she had a thin--whisper thin--bit of fabric covering her skin, but his rough palm seared into her.

Thank god they reached the booth quickly because his touch electrified her.

Austin stepped up to the table and poured her some fizzy water, adding a slice of lemon. He was leaning forward, and the black denim of his jeans stretched appealingly over his narrow hips and perfect ass.

Did he have to be so frickin' gorgeous?

He turned and presented her the drink with a flourish, his jaw relaxed and smile wide. "Here you go."

She needed to chill out. He was her boss. The Hotel Kings were one big happy family. Despite his sweet side, he was an ex-rockstar with an edge and didn't that make him even more tempting? She thought she'd kicked her bad boy habit--so much for a decade of mindfulness training.

"Thank you." To stop herself from ogling him like he was a double scoop of Nutella gelato, she dropped her gaze to her drink and took a sip.

Socializing came easy to her, but Austin had her stumbling over small talk. Time to mingle with the group. Safer that way. She glanced around, but everyone was cozied up and Brigitte was nowhere to be seen.

Maybe she'd go to the restroom and gather her composure. Mind made up; she opened her mouth to excuse herself, but Austin extended one strong hand.

"Give me your glass and come dance with me." It wasn't a question.

Heat curled down her spine. And just like that, her brilliant plan evaporated.

How dangerous could one dance be?

CHAPTER 10

He'd officially lost his ever-loving mind. But when Kenzie had sauntered in wearing a tiny dress and a gorgeous grin, his blood heated. So much for keeping his distance, but everyone else was coupled up, Brigitte was off dancing, and he'd wanted Kenzie to feel comfortable. *Yeah, sure, that's what he was doing.*

People were packed on the dance floor like sardines. He navigated through the crowd, preternaturally aware of her slender fingers intertwined with his, the coolness of her palm against his. Soon he'd be enveloped in her peachy scent, her sexy toned body would be pressed close to him, and the lines between boss and employee would blur.

When he found a sliver of space, he turned, and she was in his arms. His throat tightened when she placed her hands on his shoulders. He caught the subtle curve of her hips, forcing himself to keep his hold light.

A fast paced techno dance tune pounded around them. How the hell did people dance to this stuff? They swayed to the beat, and perspiration prickled on the back of his neck. It had to be from the press of too many bodies crammed into one room, right?

Her plump lips curved up. "This is out of control!"

He nodded, struggling to tap into his own self-control. What the hell had he been thinking asking her to dance?

Suddenly, the DJ changed the vibe with a romantic ballad—what were the odds when he was out here with Kenzie? These clubs usually spun the same monotonous techno beat all night to keep the energy high and the drinks flowing.

Shit, he was in trouble. Should he lead her off the floor and return to the group?

Kenzie wound her slender arms around his neck and tilted her head back. "Maybe the DJ saw nobody could move and made it a slow dance?" Her eyes echoed shallow tropical waters, azure and clear, cool and inviting.

Now her perfect breasts were crushed against his chest, her flat belly in line with his burgeoning hard-on. *Damn.* No way to control his body's reaction to her proximity. His hands slid around her, meeting right at the base of her spine, mere inches above her taut ass. He managed not to groan.

She sucked in a sharp inhale—no way could she ignore his cock digging into her.

But she didn't step away. Her arms tightened around him, her nipples pierced into him, and their hips rocked side to side to the tantric melody blaring through the nightclub. Unable to resist, he stroked his hands up her back, then returned to her hips, tugging her closer against him.

He gazed down at her, her tempting lips parted, her chest rising and falling in quick bursts. She was just as turned on as he was. "Kenzie."

He lowered his head and she rose on her tiptoes to meet him. He brushed his mouth against hers. Once, twice, sampling. A jolt of energy sparked down his spine.

She threaded her fingers through his hair and murmured against his mouth, "Kiss me."

He slid his hands up and clasped the back of her head, holding her in place. He slanted his mouth against hers and she opened for him, her breath mingling with his. She tasted delicious, like peaches, vanilla, and sunshine. A moan escaped her, and she swirled her tongue with his, eager and excited. She nipped his bottom lip, then deepened the kiss, digging her fingernails into his scalp.

The pulsating crowd, the booming music––all of it faded away, leaving only Kenzie and him. Every nerve ending in his body thrummed and his pulse galloped through his veins. The little sounds she was making low in her throat were driving him nuts. A wave of possessiveness filled him. He stroked his hands down her back, grabbed her ass.

He needed her now. Right now.

Suddenly two screeching girls slammed into Kenzie, knocking her out of the way, and pawed at him. "Oh my god. Austin! Austin Michaels! It's really you! Oh my god!"

He stumbled back, bumping the people behind him and checked to see if Kenzie was okay. She was a few feet away, her eyes wide, her jaw slack.

He held up his hands, smiled at the girls, and backed away. "Sorry girls, people tell me that all the time. Not me." *Damn.* Of all the times to have former groupies descend on him.

He grabbed Kenzie's hand and led her off the dance floor. Time to return to the relative safety of the table. He'd forgotten the Hollywood crowd would be more likely to recognize him. Black Velvet Machine had come up through the usual clubs––the Whiskey, the Roxy, and The Viper Room. Those same people patronized the trendy nightclubs.

Unlike some of his band mates who couldn't get enough of the women throwing themselves at them backstage, he'd never thrived on it. Those women didn't care about him, they just wanted to fuck a rockstar or say they did.

Yeah, at first the attention had been flattering and a little awe-inspiring, but it got old quick. And even if the women were nice, 99.9% of them were more interested in dating a celebrity and living the lifestyle.

Except for Chantelle, the women he'd met once the band took off seemed to care more about Austin Michaels the lead singer than Austin Michaels the man. But in the end, he'd received the tough lesson that's all she had cared about too. They'd been in love but the minute she realized he was walking away from the band, she bolted. Now she was dating some guy who starred in one of those reality real estate shows.

He followed Kenzie off the dance floor and couldn't help admiring the sway of her hips and the way her slinky dress showed off her curves. Now he'd tasted her, and he was royally screwed.

Once they'd made their escape, she dropped his hand and raised a dark blonde eyebrow. "Does that happen to you often?"

He shook his head. "Not in a while. Sorry about that."

"It's not your fault those girls are bonkers. I'll meet you back at the table after I go to the restroom."

Time to interrupt all the couples and make them socialize as a group. For Kenzie's sake. Hell, for his own sake. And if they failed to comply, he'd drag Ryan away for a whiskey shot or something.

He hadn't anticipated seeing Kenzie this weekend. Had needed the space and now he required the separation. He'd had a few cocktails and he might not be using his best judgment, so it was safer to keep his distance from her, without acting like a dick.

Because right now his dick was calling the shots and that was not okay.

When he stepped up to the booth, only his sister Dylan and her husband Gabriel were making out--much to his relief. Everyone else was chatting and laughing.

He slid into the booth next to Amanda, where there was only space for one person. When Kenzie returned from the restroom, she could sit far, far away and socialize on her own.

No way was he going to be alone with her again tonight. And no way was he venturing through the club again until they left. No more run-ins with rabid fans. Over the last year working with the hotels, he'd almost forgotten what it was like. He couldn't get out of L.A. soon enough.

"Was the dance floor as much of a nightmare as it looks?" Amanda asked. She sat cuddled up to her 6'5 firefighter husband Jake.

"Worse. I don't miss the club scene one bit." Austin reached for his scotch and downed a mouthful.

Sam leaned across Amanda with a smirk. "I saw you and Kenzie out there. You were k-i-s-s-i-n-g. I knew it."

Amanda's eyes widened. "What? You kissed her?"

"Shhh, stop yelling." He glared at Sam. "How old are you, Sam? 10? We were just dancing, okay? Your imagination is out of control." *Damn Samantha and her eagle eyes.*

Amanda laid one cool palm on his arm. "Calm down. I didn't see anything except those girls assaulting you. I'm sorry you're still dealing with that nonsense. Hopefully nobody alerts the press you're here."

The iron tight muscles on the back of his neck softened. Amanda was the eldest sister and always the voice of calm and reason--probably part of why she was such an excellent equine vet. Sam tended to blurt out whatever popped into her mind at any given moment. He usually found her hilarious, but not so much right now.

Jake nodded. "I didn't see anything except those girls and since you shut them down, I doubt they'll be calling TMZ. Do you want to switch seats, so you'll be more hidden?"

"Yeah man, thanks." His brother in law was built like Jason Momoa and would be the perfect buffer for the rest of the evening.

They swapped seats and he scooted in next to Sam and her husband Holt. He sighed and sipped his drink. What a night. Only a few more hours until he could escape what should have been a guys' night.

Sam elbowed him in the side and smirked. "I know you like her."

"Sam, stop harassing him or I'll insist we go dance." Holt wrapped his arm around her and pulled her in close.

"No way am I going out there." Sam lips curved up into a mischievous grin. "But you were in on the wager too, honey."

Holt's brow furrowed. "Sam––"

"Wager?"

"It's nothing Austin. Don't listen to Sam, she's been drinking champagne all day." Guilt flashed across Amanda's face and Jake stiffened.

He leaned in and gripped the table. "What is the wager?"

Holt sighed and glanced over his shoulder to the other end of the enormous booth where Kenzie now chatted with Phoebe and Rafe, Jake's big brother. "Okay, okay. But it's all in good fun. Don't get pissed off."

Austin drummed his fingers on the table and waited.

"Well, you know all the guys have fallen for the woman they work with so far and you're next in line…and the chemistry between the two of you is obvious." Amanda delivered the words with her sweet smile.

Seriously? "So, let me get this straight, you guys made a bet on me and Kenzie? All of you?"

Holt had the grace to look sheepish. "It's just in fun."

"Yeah, it's funny, right?" Jake's eyes widened.

"How much?" His jaw tightened.

Amanda's lips twitched. "Just $100. C'mon Austin, you're always the first one in on a bet or a practical joke. Weren't you the one giving Jack and Campbell the most crap?"

He sat back against the smooth leather seat and crossed his arms over his chest. "Sharing what I observed and making a childish wager are two different things." He sounded like a petulant child, even to his own ears.

Sam snorted. "Like you wouldn't have done it."

He narrowed his eyes. "What if she finds out? You don't think this is awkward as hell and unprofessional? Shit, she could sue us for harassment."

"Not if you don't say anything. We all really like her so just relax. You're the laidback brother, remember? And besides, we're betting on Brigitte and Lucas next," Sam said.

"Fine. But for the record, I don't like it." Hell, he sounded like his brother, who rarely had displayed his sense of humor prior to Charlie's softening him up.

Ryan and Charlie chose that moment to reappear at the booth. Charlie's dark blonde hair was mussed, and Ryan's usually serious expression had been replaced with a goofy grin. Yeah, these two couldn't keep their hands off each other, even when they were supposed to be celebrating their last night of singledom separately.

"Hey guys, I need a drink." Charlie grinned, her gaze surveying the bottle service set up for the table.

"I bet you do. We've got grapefruit juice, does a Greyhound work for you?" Austin said.

"Make it two. Thanks, little brother, you're the best." Ryan threw his arm around his fiancé and pulled her in close to his side.

Since bartending was one of his specialties, Austin got busy mixing two stiff drinks for them. Something tugged in his chest when he observed how happy his brother was with Charlie. Sure, he was still an uptight, tough CEO but she'd tempered his edges and brought out his best side. What would that feel like?

"What did we miss? Anything exciting?" Charlie asked as she accepted her cocktail.

Austin blew out a breath. "Just found out about your bet, that's all."

Ryan grimaced. "Bet?"

He pointed a finger at his big brother. "Don't play dumb with me. Let's just say you better have chosen the correct side on this one."

Holt interjected. "And some groupies spotted Austin on the dance floor, so we've got to keep him hidden."

Charlie's dark brows drew together. "Oh geez, we need a disguise for you or something. Well, you should have everything you need at the table, right? Family, friends, and vodka."

"Sure. All good. Enjoy your party." He flashed a grin. Nobody would see how he really felt. He'd just be 'happy go lucky' Austin. But damn if he didn't wish he and Kenzie were somewhere alone. Or he was out of here.

For now, staying at opposite ends of the booth would have to be enough. But once they were back in the desert, how long could he resist the pull of Mackenzie Banks?

*K*enzie tip-toed through the luxurious suite that now resembled a post-cyclone disaster area. Sparkly stilettos and brightly colored sandals sprawled on the floor like tumbleweeds in an old Western. Half-empty glasses with lipstick marks and pizza boxes were strewn on the elegant tables along with a few tiaras.

It looked more like a sorority house instead of a fancy hotel filled with professional women. She'd bonded with everyone, as Lucy had promised. Last night had been a blast and she didn't regret coming at all.

Well, except perhaps for kissing Austin on the dance floor. She pressed her fingertips against her mouth and her eyelids floated shut.

Okay, who was she kidding? It was by far the most incredible, passionate kiss she'd ever experienced. She'd forgotten where she was. Nothing had mattered except for Austin, and that was a problem. Time to high tail it back to Palm Springs and focus on work. And on avoiding him.

On the drive home, she'd compartmentalize their kiss. Before next weekend's Monterey wedding, she would fortify her boundaries where he was concerned. Because she'd crafted a detailed five-year life plan which began with The Monroe. Said future didn't include a fling with a sexy ex-rockstar.

Because if they'd been alone last night? That kiss would have ended up with them up against the wall in a secluded corner of the nightclub, with him buried inside her.

Because she really needed a one-night stand with her boss. Not. She grimaced.

She scribbled a note for the girls and placed it on the marble bar top and stepped out of the suite. She had a two hour drive by herself, which was plenty of time to listen to one of her favorite manifestation meditations and center herself. Priorities––she'd get her priorities straight once and for all. Long-term life plan over short-term pleasure.

When she walked over to the lot where she'd parked, she looked around in confusion. Her car wasn't there. She twirled in a slow circle and hurried to the end of the lot–– where she knew damn well she had not parked––but no luck. She'd parked between a silver SUV and one of those fancy low-slung sports cars. They were still there, it was 7 a.m. after all, but the space between them was vacant. Had she gotten towed?

The parking attendant had assured her the property was intended for overflow hotel parking. What the hell? She gritted her teeth and marched back to the valet station where a different uniformed guy stood.

"Can I help you, miss?" He was obviously an actor earning his living while waiting for his big break. Too handsome to be anything else. But that wasn't the point.

"I hope so. Last night the other valet told me to park next door since the hotel garage was full. And now my car isn't there."

His dark eyebrows drew together. "Are you sure?"

She closed her eyes and counted to five, then stared at him. "Yes, I am sure. Is there a way to check to see if it was towed for some reason?"

"I can do that. Hold on and I'll give the company we use a call to see if they came out last night. What type of car was it?"

"It's a white VW, License plate XTG 711. California plates." Why would her car get towed though? She'd been in a designated spot, had the ticket on the dashboard, and everything was up to date. She inhaled a deep breath.

Mr. Valet Actor dialed a number, relayed the information, and held up one hand. With a nod and a frown, he ended the call.

"I'm afraid they didn't come out at all last night. No record of towing any car from next door. Why don't I walk over with you and check. Maybe you missed it. Or maybe one of your friends moved it? Playing a prank?"

She released a long exhale but couldn't control the rising volume of her voice. "You're kidding, right? I didn't miss my car, nor do I know anyone who would move it."

"Kenzie?" A familiar voice rasped.

She turned and there he was, wearing a Queen concert-T and faded jeans, a black baseball cap shoved onto his unruly hair. *Great.*

"Hey Austin."

A crease formed between his brows. "You heading out already?"

"That was my plan, but my car is gone."

"Gone?" His indigo eyes narrowed. "Didn't you valet?"

She gestured with a thumb to the attendant. "The hotel's lot was full and the valet told me to park in the overflow lot next door and now my car is gone."

"That stinks. Did you get towed?"

"Apparently, it wasn't towed, so I'm thinking my car was stolen last night. Which is just fantastic."

Austin swung his gaze to the valet. "You guys have security cameras, right?"

"Umm…the towing company said they didn't tow anyone from here last night. I can check with my manager about the security cameras. But we don't own the lot."

"I need you to go check with your manager right now and we'll call the police in the meanwhile. You guys are a 5 star hotel, and you don't ensure that guests' cars are safe and secure? That's a problem." Austin snapped out each word.

Actor-Valet backed up, nodding his head. "Yes sir, please wait right here. I'll be right back." He backed up and scurried through the glass double-doors.

Austin angled toward her. "I was going to grab a coffee around the corner. What can I get you? Or do you want to come with?"

"Thank you. I'll wait for him to come back and call the police, but I would love a large latte with oat milk, please." Caffeine wouldn't make her car materialize, but it would help the headache throbbing at her temples.

"I'll be right back. We'll get this figured out." He smiled and strode away.

Well, wasn't it nice to have someone take charge and help her deal with the crisis? Even though she'd been leaving early specifically to avoid him? What were the odds?

What were the odds the first time she owned a car since college, it was stolen in the first month? She sank onto the charming wrought iron bench, propped her elbows on her knees and dropped her head into her hands. *Crap.*

After a few self-indulgent breaths, she pulled out her phone. Time to make a report and pray that somehow the valet was mistaken about her car getting towed. No time to deal with a stolen car. Not to mention, now how was she getting back to Palm Springs? And getting around Palm Springs once she was there? She called the cops.

By the time she gave the hotel's address to the dispatcher, Austin returned with their drinks and a large white bakery bag. She reached for the coffee. Boy did she need the kick right now because today was promising to be a long one.

Austin sat down, the heat from his muscular thigh next to her sending a shot of awareness down her spine. Yeah, their chemistry wouldn't quit.

"Yes, thanks so much. I'll be right out in front of the hotel. And hopefully we'll have some security footage." She ended the call.

"In the meantime, I figured some food would help. That is, if you eat carbs?" Austin opened the bag and tilted it toward her.

Her mouth watered. Croissants. One of her weaknesses. "Of course I eat carbs––it's all about balance. So that's for me?"

He nodded and held the bag out toward her. "They've got the best croissants in L.A., trust me. And they're still warm."

She reached into the bag and her fingers closed around the warm, flaky goodness. "Thanks." Okay, the day had improved marginally.

He crossed one ankle over his knee, sat back and sipped his coffee. "So, if your car has indeed been stolen, you can ride with me back to Palm Springs."

"Aren't you sticking around today with the guys?"

He shook his head. "Nah, we've all got a lot to do. I can head back whenever you need."

Two hours in an enclosed space with him would be dangerous, but what choice did she have? Unless miraculously her car reappeared, which was highly unlikely. "Okay, once I've given the cops the report, I'll be ready to go whenever you are. I appreciate it."

"Do you want me to wait with you for the police?"

This sweet considerate side of him was disarming. Not what she needed after the memory of their scorching kiss. Damn it, she wasn't just attracted to Austin; she liked him.

"No, I'm packed and ready to go. I'd rather get on the road as soon as possible." She gestured to her scarlet leather duffel bag sitting on the ground beside them.

"Always efficient. I like that about you. I'll go grab my stuff." With a lazy grin, he rose, and stretched his arms overhead.

The hem of his t-shirt lifted, exposing a narrow expanse of flat, hard abs and a treasure trail of hair disappearing into his jeans. Her mouth grew parched. She quickly lowered her gaze and gulped her latte before she gaped at him like a fish. Damn, he was too sexy. Add that to him stepping in to help her, and she was in trouble.

"It is my superpower." She winked and waved one hand. *Keep it light, girl.*

He sauntered toward the entrance just as a police cruiser turned onto the street. She may or may not have admired his perfect ass the whole way.

The cruiser parked at the curb and a young stocky officer with close cropped brown hair exited the car. "You Ms. Banks?"

She rose and hurried over. "I am. Thanks for coming so quickly."

She spent the next twenty minutes with yet another man questioning if she was sure she'd parked in the lot. Once the report was filed, the policeman took off with a final comment warning her not to get her hopes up.

The valet-actor returned, and his cheeks were brick red. "Ms. Banks, I'm afraid I have some bad news. We usually do have security footage, but someone broke the cameras last night. There's no footage after 8 p.m. and we learned a car is missing from the hotel's garage too."

What could she say? It wasn't her day.

Austin strode out of the lobby with a gunmetal gray backpack. "Any luck?"

"I'd say that would be a resounding no. Apparently another car is gone, and the thieves broke the security cameras." At least she hadn't left anything in the trunk.

"That sucks. Do you want to call your insurance company now or wait until we're back in the desert?"

"I thought I'd just call from your car on the way. You know, to save time?" She shrugged one shoulder.

"I don't have my car. I rode my bike."

Her mouth dropped open. "Your motorcycle?"

Anxiety swirled through her. Motorcycles reminded her of an adrenaline junkie ex-boyfriend who loved to weave through rush hour traffic and pop wheelies. The one time she'd agreed to a ride, he'd blasted through the sound barrier. Or it felt like it anyway.

That was their final date.

"Yeah, I take it whenever I can. She's a beauty and lucky for you, I carry an extra helmet."

"But motorcycles on the highway are dangerous." She shook her head and backed away from him.

"It's less than two hours, I'm an excellent driver and I promise to get you back to The Monroe in one piece. You aren't scared, are you?" His midnight eyes widened.

"You might be a good driver but what about everybody else? People drive like maniacs in California. Maybe I should call an Uber."

"Kenzie, an Uber would be really expensive. I promise I'll go the speed limit. The Heritage Classic is sturdy--one of the best bikes out there. You might even enjoy it."

She wiped her now slick palms on her jeans and struggled

to regulate her accelerated breathing. It wasn't like she was a chicken, but motorcycles scared her. People had phobias about all kinds of things--this was one of hers.

Fate had thrown them together again. Now she'd be pressed against Austin, hurtling down the highway on a death machine. But he was right, the practical thing to do-- and she prided herself on being practical--was to put on her big girl panties.

How bad could it be?

"Fine. But you'll drive the speed limit and no tricks." Yes, she sounded like a grandmother and didn't care.

His lips twitched and he held up both hands. "Yes, ma'am. Come on, let's go. And I'll only pop a few wheelies."

She rolled her eyes and couldn't resist smiling. "Yeah right. Not on my watch, Michaels."

"I'm in the hotel garage. Benefit of the bike is there's almost always room to park." He glanced at her apologetically. "They'll find your car, don't worry."

They descended to the first level of the garage where a shiny cream and black Harley awaited them. The bike looked solid enough--for something with two wheels and an engine. Austin pulled two silver metallic helmets from the saddlebags, stowed their bags inside, and climbed on the machine.

The helmet was like a snowboarding helmet. But she hesitated, nibbling on the inside of her cheek while she fiddled with the strap.

Austin patted the ebony leather seat behind him. "Did you want to get back to Palm Springs today or...?"

"I'm coming. Just hold on." Thank god she'd worn her high tops and a pair of old jeans instead of shorts. Small blessings and all that.

She crossed to the motorcycle and swung one leg over, placing one hand lightly on his shoulder for balance. She nestled up against all those lean muscles, her legs framing his. A now familiar punch of energy shot through her, and heat bloomed in her center.

His strong artist's hands gripped the handlebars. "Wrap your arms around me. I promise I'll make the ride good for you." They burst out of the dimly lit garage into the sunny California morning.

Once he hit the road, he revved the engine and they were soaring past rows of closed restaurants and clubs, toward Highway 10. Her thighs gripped his legs like a vice and a crowbar couldn't pry her arms from around his waist. Time to employ her yogic skills to divert her attention to the beautiful morning and away from her short-circuiting hormones.

Because being flush against him reminded her of lying in bed fantasizing about how he'd feel up close. Reality beat her imagination and it took effort not to stroke her hands along his six-pack or lower.

At least he couldn't see her expression, nor could they have a conversation. Maybe in a hundred miles or so she'd have found her equilibrium. Or melted into a puddle. From lust, not the searing heat.

Once he eased onto the freeway, she closed her eyes. Seeing all the cars and 18-wheelers whizzing by would only stoke her fear. Instead, she rested her cheek against his back and held on to his hot, hard body and chose to trust him. He hadn't let her down so far.

His expert handling of the bike softened the tension in her jaw. His masterful swerves and turns evoked the same feeling like when they'd swayed to the music last night. Like they were one with the machine. And damn if the roar of the engine between her legs combined with being plastered to Austin like a barnacle didn't turn her on. As if she needed more incentive to jump his bones.

No way could she ever admit she found riding his bike

sexy. Nor would she admit that the speed thrilled her too. But ohmygod, between the humming of the bike and the feel of him, she could probably orgasm before they arrived back at the hotel. So much for her brilliant plan to evade him at all costs.

CHAPTER 12

$\mathcal{A}$ustin could count the times he'd cried on one hand. The first few occasions occurred when he was nine years old, and his policeman dad was killed in the line of duty. The next time, he'd been thrown from a horse after he'd moved to Pacific Vista Ranch with his mom and brothers. He'd been eleven.

And he'd never admit this to a single, solitary soul but he'd cried in eighth grade when the girl he was madly in love with, Marielle Dawn, stopped speaking to him after he'd written her a poem and then started hanging with his best friend. Former best friend. The jerk.

That was the last time he'd cried over a woman.

Early on, he'd learned humor helped him navigate tough times. If he joked and acted like he was fine, eventually he would be. When Tommy died a few years back, his go-to tactic failed him. Six months passed in a numb fog before, like a waking limb, feeling returned along with an endless well of tears.

When he'd finally crashed, the emotional storm had raged for an entire weekend. He'd returned to Pacific Vista Ranch and stayed in the guest house for about a month. Between the unconditional love from his mom, and the soothing peace of the secluded ranch, he had recovered. Mostly.

Right now, as he cruised his bike into a parking spot at The Monroe?

He could sob like a newborn baby––the last two hours had been excruciating torture. Holy hell. Kenzie had been flush against his back, her long toned legs and slender arms squeezing him tight. Any time a truck or a speeding vehicle approached, each tantalizing limb crushed him like a python pulverizing its prey. Even through his light jacket and shirt, her breasts had jabbed holes into his back. He'd been hard as steel for the entire drive.

Time to dive into an ice cold shower. Again.

The moment he released the kickstand, Kenzie scrambled off the bike. She backed away and ripped off the helmet. Wayward strands of strawberry blonde hair stuck up in all directions. Was that what she'd look like waking up beside him?

Yeah, his imagination wasn't helping his predicament.

"We made it." She placed the helmet on the Harley's seat. "Can I get my bag, please?"

He stepped off and opened the saddlebags. "You're all set. That wasn't so bad, was it?" *More like the seventh ring of hell, but whatever.* He grinned at her, mindful to keep his own duffel bag in front of him. No need for her to see he was at half-mast.

"We're alive and made it back before lunch, so thanks." She grabbed her leather duffle bag and pivoted away. "Gotta run, see you later."

He removed his helmet and scrubbed his hands through his hair and admired the way her dark denim lovingly cupped her curves. Were her obvious nerves from the motorcycle or from their two hour embrace? After last night's kiss, the bike ride only emphasized their explosive chemistry.

No more motorcycle rides. If she needed to go somewhere, she could borrow his car. Or hell, he'd hire a car service for her. Safer that way.

Time to take that shower so he could attempt to focus on work the remainder of the day. He strode through the unfinished lobby to his suite, working to regulate his unsteady breath. He stripped off his sweaty clothes, leaving a trail to the bathroom in his wake.

He opened the shower's glass door, flipped on the water, and stepped under the enormous rain-showerhead. His shoulders relaxed as the spray pounded his back, soothing the rigid muscles. He soaped up, took himself in hand and with the recent visceral memory of Kenzie's tight graceful body pressed against his back, took a mere six strokes to completion.

Yeah, he hadn't gotten laid in months. He'd had a few casual hook-ups after learning his ex-girlfriend had dated him for a year solely because he was famous. The experience hadn't exactly left him eager to dive into another relationship.

And then both his brothers had found their true loves, and Jack and Campbell and Lucy and Cameron were all heading to the altar. Although it was funny they were betting on him and Kenzie following the Hotel Kings tradition of falling for your employee, he'd already loved and lost, thank you very much.

Losing his dad and his best friend taught him not to rely on the long-term.

Especially since he had transitioned from the band to the hotel gig. No more purging through his music. He hadn't been able to write one single lyric since Tommy died. Hadn't been able to pour out his emotions on the page anymore.

And so, he had to keep everything light and fun in his personal life.

Although if he were being honest with himself, he'd have to admit that Kenzie Banks stirred his heart. Deeper than he'd experienced since before Tommy's overdose.

He banged his forehead against the smooth tile wall, then turned off the water, and stepped out of the shower. No, no, no. He was just horny. He'd be smart to see if he could find some local woman who wanted something casual. Yeah, no strings attached, a friends with benefits arrangement. Once the physical edge was handled, he'd be fine.

Although he hadn't been attracted to anyone in the months before his new Spa Manager showed up and how would someone else compare? Crap. He muttered under his breath as he massaged his hair with the soft cotton towel. He dropped it to the floor and braced both hands on the sink's vanity and looked himself in the eyes.

"Admit it to yourself, dude. You want her. You want her badly. And you can't risk fucking things up by catching feelings. So, get a grip and get to work." Great, now he was talking to himself.

He hadn't even done that before heading onstage to perform at a sold-out Wembley Stadium show when he'd suffered an uncharacteristic bout of stage fright. But one peach scented, perfectionistic yoga teacher reduced him to a hormone-raging teenager. He rolled his eyes at his reflection and stalked to the closet

Time to tackle his mile-long to-do list.

He snatched up a pair of board shorts and his favorite Pearl Jam concert t-shirt. Time to get busy. Although the crew took Sundays off, he needed to review the latest plans before Craig and the guys arrived at O'Dark thirty Monday morning. It was a short work week because they were headed to Monterey on Friday, but Craig could always call him if there was an issue.

But the real issue was instead of getting space from Kenzie to fortify his defenses, she'd be his damn "date" and close by for three days.

On the private plane.

At the wedding.

At the resort where friends and family were staying.

All. Freakin'. Weekend.

He strode to his desk, flipped open his laptop, and put in his Air Pods with some mellow acoustic tunes. Time to get shit done.

KENZIE HUNG up the phone after spending a scintillating hour talking to the insurance adjustor and assuring the suspicious old biddy that yes, she hadn't forgotten where she parked her car and no, one of her friends hadn't borrowed it without telling her. Between the cop's questions and the insurance company's insinuations, she felt like she was the one under investigation for theft, not the actual thief. Sheesh.

Basically, the adjustor told her, without actually telling her, that her car was long gone. Apparently, her model was popular with thieves because resale parts had high value. Lovely. That would have been a handy tidbit of information to have prior to purchasing the vehicle.

At least Austin had offered to lend her his vintage Mustang. As long as he was not in the car with her, she should be okay.

And she certainly was never, ever, ever riding on Austin's Harley again. Not because she'd been scared of an accident but because it was one of the arousing experiences of her life. Even after a quick dip in the pool upon their return, she wouldn't be able to erase the feel of his hot hard body from her memory anytime in the next century.

Now to avoid him for the next four days and fortify her defenses before the private plane and proximity to him all weekend. At least she'd bonded with everyone at the party last night. So, she'd just make sure to always be in the group. Easy. Her heart kicked against her ribs

She bolted up out of her chair. Who was she kidding? Her nerves were wound tight and when she felt out of control like this, yoga was the only way to tame the pack of wild monkeys racing around in her mind. Yoga helped her eliminate distractions––even a 6 foot 1 gorgeous one––and sink into her body and her breath. No way could she tackle her weekly planning until she'd settled her mind.

She'd already changed into a pair of shorts and flowy tank top. She unrolled her purple yoga mat, so it faced the floor-to-ceiling windows and placed a pair of soft foam blocks beside it. She pressed play on a fun Vinyasa playlist she'd titled "Badass Chicks" which featured everyone from Gwen Stefani to Stevie Nicks to Florence and the Machine.

She stood at the top of her mat in Tadasana or Mountain pose, palms pressed together at her heart, and closed her eyes. Three cleansing breaths, inhaling through her nose and exhaling through her mouth. Breathing in light and joy and exhaling shadow and stress. A visual of Austin's beautiful mouth lowering toward hers flashed on the dark screen of her eyelids. Her eyes flew open and she re-focused on the jagged mountains silhouetted against the unrelieved blue canvas of sky.

Focus on the breath. Filter out the rest.

She inhaled and swept her arms overhead, exhaled and swan dived forward, inhaled half-way lift and exhaled floating back to chatarangua dandasana. Upward facing dog back to her first downward dog. Immediately, her muscles and bones sighed in relief at the familiar routine, her breath steadied. Home--her yoga mat was home. The small world where all that mattered was how she felt and everything else could recede until her mind cleared, and her heart softened.

An hour later, she sprawled on her mat, savoring every second of Savasana, yoga's final resting pose. She'd replaced her frayed nerves with relaxed muscles and a calm mind. Now, she was finally ready to tackle her daily plan.

She rose, rolled up the mat, and stowed it into the closet. Her stomach growled. She hadn't eaten today besides the croissant and her blood sugar had plummeted. She strode to her purse, ready to grab her keys to head to the store and stock up her mini refrigerator for the week, and halted in her tracks.

Damn it. No car. The logical thing to do would be to borrow Austin's car. But right now, she was chicken to see him. Maybe she should order delivery and deal with it in the morning. But she was out of coffee and oat milk and basically everything.

And wasn't this ludicrous? She'd simply stroll over there, ask to borrow the car from the doorway where it was safe. He'd offered, right? She needed to implement her self-control and act professional. Starting now.

Well, starting in a few hours. For now, she'd order a salad with grilled shrimp from one of the delicious little spots she'd discovered. After she finished her tasks and had fortified herself, she'd approach Austin and ask for the car keys.

Resolved, she picked up her phone. Her plan was sensible, and she'd pull it off without a hitch. Her yoga session had soothed her, and she'd be fine.

Keep telling yourself that, Kenzie.

CHAPTER 13

*A*ustin reclined against the mound of pillows on his King sized bed and cradled his beloved guitar. After finishing up reams of really fucking boring paperwork, he needed time to refuel.

Since he'd quit the band, it hurt too much to play Black Velvet Machine's songs--mostly written by him and Tommy. Instead, he'd play some of his favorite musicians' songs. Some Chris Cornell, some Eddie Vedder, some Killers, some classics like Led Zeppelin.

Once or twice, he'd picked up a notebook and attempted to spark a new song. Anything at all. But his well was dry-- he hadn't written a single lyric or crafted a solitary melody since Tommy's death. Maybe he never would again. Writer's block was real.

A knock sounded at the door and jolted him out of his brooding. He set his guitar down and strolled over. When he opened it, his mind sputtered and blanked.

Kenzie's strawberry-blond hair was slicked back into a ponytail leaving her lovely face bare. Her lithe figure was encased in yoga pants and a tank top. He shoved his hands in his pockets, so he didn't grab her and toss her over his shoulder, fireman style.

"Hey." Yeah, that's all he had. Hadn't she gotten the memo to avoid him?

She cleared her throat and gave a small smile. "I'm sorry to bug you again but any way I can borrow your car? I need to pick up some groceries."

Her husky voice slammed into him like a punch to the gut. "Do you want me to drive you?"

"Oh no, you've already done enough. And I have a process at the store. You might find it annoying." Her lips twitched.

And just like that, the tension tightening his shoulders relaxed. "Let me guess, you've got an excel spreadsheet for your grocery list?"

"Ha ha. Not a spreadsheet. But I may or may not have it divided by type of food." A flush of pink stained her high cheekbones.

He chuckled––could she be any cuter? "Of course you do. More efficient to hit those aisles in order. You crack me up."

She shrugged one shoulder, and her smile grew sheepish. "At least I'm up front about my geekiness. I'm happy to pick things up for you."

He hated grocery shopping. "That would be great. Hold on, I'll grab the keys and jot down what I need. Okay if it isn't in alphabetical order?"

She rolled her eyes. "I'll integrate it into mine, don't worry. I'm an expert."

"Come on in and have a seat. I'll just be a minute."

He hurried to his desk, scribbled down a few essentials, all the while hyperaware of her peachy fragrance and long limbs. He blew out an exhale and turned.

She stood at the windows, staring out at the early evening sky, a canvas streaked with an explosion of violet and lemon and tangerine. "Every day I'm falling more and more for the beauty of this place."

Something tugged in his chest, but he shoved it aside. "Yeah, the desert is growing on me too. Here you go. It's a baby blue Mustang, parked next to my bike."

She turned and took the keys and the list, without quite meeting his gaze. "Great, thanks again. Be back in a few."

When the door closed behind her, he remained rooted to the spot. Something about her drew him in and it wasn't the physical package. Something about her wounds, her thin veneer of control shown as organization, hinted at emotional depths beneath her polished surface. And that passion had been in full force last night on the dance floor. The way she'd felt in his arms, the way she'd tasted when they kissed, the way her arms hugged him on his Harley today had felt natural. Felt right.

He massaged the tight muscles on the back of his neck. Unlike his brother Ryan, who was a master of self-control and reserved revealing emotion for his inner circle, he'd shared his with millions through lyrics and music. Somehow singing about heartbreak was easier than sharing even a hint of what he was feeling. Kenzie triggered emotions he hadn't allowed himself in years.

He was intuitive and experienced enough to know she was affected by him too. Until the hotel opened and more employees were around, avoiding each other would be tough. Who was he trying to kid? Day by day was the only way to move forward.

For now, he'd jam on his guitar to a song that would definitely get him out of the mood to pounce on Ms. Mackenzie Banks upon her return. Time for a little Alice in Chains to cement his mood to melancholy instead of romantic.

~

KENZIE PARKED Austin's perfectly restored Mustang and paused to gather her composure before delivering his groceries and keys. She was absolutely not focusing on how sitting in Austin's car made her feel closer to him. How a hint of his clean masculine scent clung to the upholstery. Now all she had to do was see him one more time today, act nonchalant, and escape to her own suite and lock the door behind her.

When she was close to him, it was nearly impossible to recall all the reasons why hooking up with him was a terrible idea. So, she'd keep minimizing their time together. Even though that plan had crashed and burned spectacularly so far.

With a snort, she stepped out of the car, grabbed the two bags––one for each of them––and marched to his door. She had this in the bag. Ha ha, had it in the bag. Oh my god, was she losing her marbles or what?

She lifted her hand to knock and before her knuckles connected with the door, a haunting melody floated to her ears and her arm dropped by her side. She set the bags on the stone walkway and leaned one shoulder against the wall, closed her eyes and allowed the beautiful notes to wash over her. Austin's guitar playing evoked sorrow and loss.

For a few moments, she simply enjoyed his magical talent and absorbed the music. Thank god he hadn't added lyrics because the song already reached its fingers inside her chest and squeezed her heart. Just like the last time she'd heard him play. When silence filled the air again, her eyes popped open, and she shook herself back to the present.

More shaken than she cared to admit, she rapped on the door. The sooner she high tailed it back to the safety and quiet of her suite, the better.

"It's unlocked." Austin's raspy voice called. She glanced down and noticed he'd propped the door on the safety latch.

She took a cleansing breath and pushed the door open.

Austin perched on the edge of the King sized bed, his dark hair in wild disarray, his cheeks pale. When he glanced up, his midnight blue gaze snared hers. Despite the several feet of distance between them, his sheer presence struck her like a lightning bolt.

She froze, her limbs heavy.

"Thanks for the groceries." His voice was neutral. Subdued compared to his usually light-hearted attitude.

He rose and prowled toward her like a sinewy panther tracking his evening meal. Was he stalking her? Or was her imagination short-circuiting?

Her tongue was as frozen as her feet. *Say something for god's sake, girl.*

"What was that song you were playing?" Ugh, not that. Why couldn't she have just handed off the groceries and fled, as planned? Why didn't her usual self-control apply with this man?

His brows flew up to his hairline. "Seriously? I'm losing my touch if you didn't recognize it."

"You know I haven't listened to a lot of alternative rock before." Although she had a feeling that was about to change.

"It's called 'Down in a Hole', by Alice in Chains. It's dark but one of my favorites."

"I could feel it. I have heard of them. Didn't the lead singer overdose?" She bit her lip. *Way to go, Mackenzie.*

"Yeah. Reminds me of Tommy." He stood a few feet from her, the strain around his sculpted lips and the fatigue in his eyes apparent.

"I'm sorry. I know grief is like a rollercoaster. Do you want to talk about it?" She may not have lost a loved one, but her parents' addictions and lack of love could still bring her down. Despite all the yoga and meditation.

"Not so much." He shook his head. "I think you said yoga helped you process your stuff; music does that for me. But I don't think you ever truly recover from losing someone too soon."

Her heart clenched and she stepped closer. "I don't think so. But maybe the pain recedes over time, or the bouts of sadness grow farther apart."

His gaze locked with hers, hurt apparent in the indigo depths. "Maybe. I lost my dad when I was 9 and sometimes it still feels like yesterday."

Emotions pulsated in the air between them. An overwhelming urge to comfort him, to lift the sorrow from his eyes, poured through her. "I'm a really good listener."

"Talking really doesn't help me much. It's either music or..." His gaze lowered to her parted lips.

"Austin?" Her legs trembled and her pulse thundered through her veins.

With a growl, he hauled her against his chest and swooped down to plunder her mouth. With a deep moan, she wound her arms around his neck and plunged her fingers into his silky hair. He stroked his strong hands up her back. Flames danced along her skin.

One hand clasped the back of her head, holding her in place.

He nipped her lower lip, then soothed it with his tongue before deepening the kiss. He smelled like soap and aroused male, a potent combination. Their surroundings faded away and Austin became her entire world. Her nipples could cut glass and were crushed against his solid chest, and her center dug into his muscular thigh. Her hips rocked into his powerful leg, the friction tantalizing.

More, she wanted more of him.

He tilted her head to the side and lightly scraped his teeth along her neck, then bit the sensitive spot where her neck met her shoulder. Her back bowed and she ground against him. "Austin," she breathed.

"Tell me what you want, beautiful." He continued to nibble down her body and captured her taut nipple between his teeth. "Do you like when I use my mouth on you?"

Her center liquefied and she almost orgasmed from the combination of his voice purring against her, even through the gossamer-thin fabric of her top. "Yes, don't stop."

He murmured his approval, sliding one hand up to cup her breast, brushing his thumb against her sensitive peak. "Don't stop what? Tell me what you want. I'll give you anything you ask."

Any remaining resistance tumbled out of her brain. Here was his bad boy side––he was a talker and damn if that wasn't her kryptonite. "More. Please more. Everything. Use your hands and your mouth and your–"

His hand splayed on her bottom, and he ground the steel ridge of his erection against her. Her head lolled back in pleasure. "My what?"

"Your cock. I want you inside me. Please Austin." Heat flashed across her entire body.

"God babe, you're a dream come true." With one swift movement, he swept her up in his arms and crossed to his bed. He stopped and looked in her eyes, his square jaw tight, his eyes hooded. "You're sure you want this. Want me."

"Yes." She'd never craved a man this way.

With a groan, he dropped her on the bed and whipped off his shirt, exposing the expanse of tanned, lean muscle she'd admired at the pool. He was a work of art. Then he shoved off his board shorts and his erection sprang free.

She ran her tongue along her upper lip. "You're beautiful."

He gave a short harsh laugh. "You're the beautiful one.

And I want to see every inch of you. Take off your clothes. Now." He stood above her, each word a sensuous command.

"You're awfully bossy." Goosebumps flared along every inch of her skin and anticipation shot to her core.

"Now or I'll tear them off." He knelt one leg on the bed and braced his hands on the firm mattress. His gaze never left hers.

"I like this outfit, hold on." She tugged her tank top over her head and tossed it aside.

Heat flared in his eyes, and he trailed his long blunt fingers across her nipples. "Your breasts are perfect. The bottoms."

She dug her heels into the bed and lifted her hips, shimmying the soft fabric down her legs. "Lucky for you I wasn't wearing panties either."

"Fuck, you are perfect." He dropped his other knee onto the bed and knelt over her, his gaze roaming over her flushed skin.

"Please touch me. Kiss me." *Fuck me.*

"Your wish is my command." He bracketed her waist with his arms and lowered his head to capture her mouth.

She moaned and swirled her tongue with his. She reached for him, eager to touch his smooth bronze flesh. Without lifting his mouth from hers, he captured both wrists in one hand and pressed them overhead. She arched up, eager for more.

His free hand clasped one breast and pinched her nipple, and sensation flooded her. He trailed his hand down along her ribcage, stroked her waist and belly, then cupped her.

"Austin," she murmured against his delicious mouth. "Please."

"Anything for you." He pressed his palm against her clit and stroked along her seam before plunging two fingers into her.

They moaned together. His guitarist fingers stroked her in a steady rhythm. Holy crap, she'd never been able to come this way, but his talented hands had her on the edge already.

"You're so wet. So ready for me. You're going to come so many times tonight, you won't be able to walk tomorrow. Now. Come now, baby." He growled the command against her mouth, his grip on her wrists tightening, the pressure of his hard-on digging into her hip.

He twisted his fingers and pressed upward, exerted the perfect pressure with his palm, and fireworks exploded in her mind, and she shattered. "Austin, Austin, ohmygod." He didn't stop until she was still.

He released her wrists, shifted back onto his knees. He spread her legs further apart, opening her to his gaze. His lips curved up in a satisfied grin. "You're so sweet, I have to taste you now."

Perspiration cloaked her skin as he slid his hands along the inside of her thighs. He lowered his head and settled his shoulders between her legs. "I'm going to kiss you here but only if you want it." His heated breath teased her, and her hips bucked.

"You know I do. Please."

He slid his hands underneath her and clasped her ass in his hands and held her immobile, then licked her in one long stroke before playing her with his talented mouth.

Her body shook and tremors began again, every inch of her on fire. She grasped his head and held on while wave after wave of pleasure washed over her. Her head dropped back on the soft mountain of pillows and every inch of her went limp. He'd wrung her out.

He nibbled his way back up her body, taking his time, his tongue lazy and teasing now. Savoring her like she was his favorite dessert. Or prey. He kissed her, slow and languorous and she tasted herself on his lips.

She reached one hand up and stroked his jaw. "My turn. I want to please you now."

"Oh, you've pleased me alright. But right now, if I'm not inside you in the next minute, I might die."

She laughed, which was a first for her during sex. "Aren't you dramatic?"

He winked and rolled off her in one smooth motion. He grabbed a condom from the nightstand, tore it open, and returned to kneel between her legs.

"Let me." Without breaking their gaze, she sheathed his steel hard cock, then brushed her fingers along his balls.

He hissed and his eyes drifted shut, those long eyelashes fanning out on his chiseled cheekbones. "Will you let me take charge?"

"Like you haven't been already. Yes."

"I need to take you hard." His eyes were hooded, his jaw tight. "Will you tell me if it's too much?"

"Mmm-hmm. I want you, Austin."

His pupils flared and he positioned himself at her entrance. He entered her in one powerful stroke, filling her completely, stretching her limits.

He held still for a moment and dropped his forehead against hers. "Okay?" He bit out the word between clenched teeth.

She clenched her inner muscles around him, reveling in the sheer size of him. She pressed her mouth to his. "I love the way you feel inside me."

He shifted onto his forearms, his gaze intense. He began to move in long powerful strokes, pulling almost all the way out and slamming back into her over and over again. Sounds of their flesh slapping together, the slickness of sweat on their skin, and the feel of him taking her hard overwhelmed her. Pleasure filled her and when he lifted one leg over his shoulder and started pounding into her, the angle made her scream his name.

"Come for me again." He gritted out the words, between each stroke.

As if on command, her body obeyed. When he reached one hand down and stroked her where they were connected, she went molten, the orgasm rocketing through her. "Yes, ohmygod yes."

His chest rumbled, and he fucked her harder and deeper than she'd ever experienced. She raked her fingernails down his back, her climax still shimmering through her. She grabbed his ass, and he shot over the edge with a roar. He went still, then turned his head and pressed an open-mouthed kiss on her cheek. "Wow."

Her lips curved up and she stroked her hands down his back, enjoying his weight on top of her. "Wow is right. I can't feel my toes."

He rolled to one side, taking her with him, still inside her. "Toes are over-rated I hear."

She smacked his butt, enjoying the rapid transition from wild sex to amused attraction. "I need my toes, thank you very much."

He grinned, pressed a light kiss on the tip of her nose, then rose. "It'll come back, don't worry."

She admired the long lean lines of his body stalking to the bathroom. He truly resembled a panther, sleek and powerful, and *holy shit* was he bossy.

And oh, did she love the bossiness. At least in bed.

She pressed her damp hair away from her face and drew her knees up to her chest. She wiggled her toes and pins and needles prickled through her.

He returned, still naked, and slid back into the bed. "Stay with me tonight."

Her breath hitched. "But the groceries and--"

He pressed one finger against her lips. "Please. I'll put them in my fridge. Stay."

When he was so sweet, how could she refuse? She wanted to stay. Wanted to savor this intimacy that felt so natural between them. Because once she left the cocoon of his room…staving off reality was an excellent idea.

"Okay. But let me up first." She had to pee.

"Deal." He rose and padded to where she'd dropped the groceries. "I've got it handled. Meet me back in bed."

When she returned, he held up the soft white sheet for her to slide in next to him. His eyes were heavy-lidded, his smile satisfied. "Come snuggle with me, beautiful."

Nerves flickered through her, but she tucked them away in the vault. Tonight, she would practice what she preached––living in the present moment. No way could she resist him, at least not tonight.

"You don't snore, do you?" She teased as she joined him under the covers. He enveloped her in his embrace, and every rock hard inch of him was imprinted on her back.

He skimmed his nose along her jaw and murmured, "Not that I know of. Feel free to wake me up for any reason, though."

He slid one hand and rested it possessively on her belly. Yeah, it wasn't his snoring that would wake her up, it would be those talented fingers.

She rested her head against his firm shoulder, enjoying how they fit together like two halves of a whole. A perfect pair.

For tonight anyway.

CHAPTER 14

*A*ustin groaned and resisted opening his eyes––he was in that space between sleep and waking. In dreamland, Kenzie's fingers wrapped around him, and her mouth teased and licked him. And felt so real.

He reached one hand down and encountered a mass of silky hair. He cracked open one eye, and there she was––no dream. Possibly the best wakeup call he'd ever had. "Kenzie."

She took her time before lifting her head and gazed up at him with those mermaid eyes. "Good morning. Just lie back and relax, this won't hurt a bit. Feel free to watch." Her voice was throaty. Every muscle in his body clenched.

Fuck. He reached for another pillow, propping his head up. "I don't know about relaxing. Your mouth feels unbelievable."

She flashed a wicked smile, then licked him from base to tip, like he was dessert. His hips jerked, eager for more. "You like that, don't you?"

"I love it." His breath hissed out when she tightened her grip and stroked him.

"I'm going to make you come fast and hard." She gazed at

him for a beat, promise in her eyes, then licked him one more time. Teasing. Taunting. Torturing him.

He fisted her hair in his hand but forced himself to maintain a semblance of control and not thrust all the way down her throat. His pulse thundered in his temples and their skin grew slick.

"Please." Her breath was heated against his skin or hell, maybe he was on fire.

"Please what?" Parroting his demands from last night. And didn't he love her taking charge now.

"Please wrap that beautiful mouth around my cock and take me deep."

Her pink lips curved up before she swallowed him, all the way. Searing pleasure surged through him, he dropped his head back onto the pillows, and received. And damn, she worked him instinctually, like he'd given her a manual.

Way too soon, his spine began to tingle, to burn, and with one talented swirl of her tongue, his back bowed off the bed and he shattered.

She took her time kissing her way up his torso until she pressed her talented mouth to his. He slid one hand down to her hips, tugged her tight into his side, and deepened the kiss.

He pulled back and stroked her damp hair away from her face. Her cheeks were flushed, and her lips were swollen and wet. "Well, I know officially today is going to be the best day of my life, no matter what happens later."

She tapped one slender finger against his lips and giggled. "A true Monday morning miracle, right?"

"Don't remind me it's Monday." He savored the feel of her pebbled nipples along his skin, the heat from one silky thigh thrown over his. "Your mouth is a true miracle. Now it's my turn to make you scream out my name."

She pressed her palm against him. "I enjoyed going down on you. You don't have to--"

"Shh, don't you think I loved tasting you last night? That I don't crave more of you?" He gripped her waist and pulled her on top of him.

Her flush deepened and her eyes floated shut. She couldn't possibly be embarrassed, could she? After last night and the morning so far? "I don't know."

"Oh, I do. And I will. Right now." He pulled her head down to meet his mouth. Nipped her full lower lip.

She rocked against him. "Well, if you insist. I mean, the sun's just rising, right?"

With a quick move, he flipped them, so she was on her back. He traced his mouth along her soft skin, inhaling her peachy scent melded with the mixture of their time together. He worked his way down her body, stopping to sample her breasts, and down along her toned belly. Anticipation bubbled through him--he was going to drive her wild.

A blast sounded from the nightstand. His frickin' phone blowing up before dawn. His hands tightened on her hips. It was too early for work--he'd ignore it.

He spread her legs apart, nuzzling the skin along her inner thighs. He glanced up and Kenzie's head lolled on the pillow, her eyes closed, her breath coming in short bursts. Oh yeah, he was going to enjoy this.

BLAAAARE. This time, Kenzie jolted up onto her elbows. "It might be an emergency. You should pick up."

He squeezed his eyes shut and blew out an exasperated exhale. It better be a damn emergency. With a muttered curse, he scooted back and reached for his phone. When he glanced at his screen, he saw it was Craig for the second time. And it was 5:30 a.m. Yeah, these early mornings were bull-shit. He was used to closing a bar at that time, not waking up.

"Everything okay?" Because it better be an emergency. The crew was arriving in an hour, which was already brutal as far as he was concerned.

"Hey Austin, sorry to bug you but there's gonna be an issue today and we need to make some shifts in the schedule."

He swung his legs over the edge of the bed and propped his elbows on his knees. "What's the issue?" So much for miraculous Monday.

"Well, remember I told you we could get major heat waves in the summer? Where the temps are into the 120s?"

"Yeah." His foreman was calling at the ass crack of dawn to discuss the weather?

"Well, instead of it happening in July, it's supposed to hit 122 by noon today."

"122 degrees, are you shitting me? So, you're saying the crew doesn't want to come to work? We're focusing on guest room interiors, right?"

"Well, yeah. And there's work we can do inside, even though the air-conditioning isn't all wired throughout those suites yet, as long as we've got the fans. But that's not the problem. We were supposed to receive more paint via FedEx today and I got a notification the airport is shut down today and possibly tomorrow."

"Huh? The airport?" He massaged the back of his neck, which was now strung as tight as his guitar.

Kenzie laid one hand on his shoulder. He glanced sideways at her, and she widened her eyes. He held up one finger and hit speaker phone.

Craig chuckled. "I forgot you're from the coast. In the summer, there's usually a few days when it's too hot for planes to land in Palm Springs because the wheels will melt on the tarmac. I don't recall it happening in May, but here we are. We've got to reschedule today and tomorrow's projects and shift the guys to other items. Can you meet me in 15?"

Austin's gritted his teeth. "I'll meet you at 6 in my office. We'll get it sorted."

"If it makes you feel any better, I grabbed donuts and coffee just the way you like it. Extra-large."

"Appreciate it. See you in a few." He powered off the phone and fell back onto the bed and covered his eyes with one arm.

Kenzie got up and searched for her clothes. He peeked, admiring her very fine ass when she bent over and picked up her shorts.

He patted the mattress. "Wait, we've got a little time. Come back here."

She tugged on her shorts and glanced back over her shoulder. "I should go back to my room before the workers arrive."

"Want to hop in the shower with me? I'll make it worth your while." He rose and stalked over to her. Yeah, him on his knees and her slick, slippery body open for him under the spray.

"Austin, no. It's going to be an intense day. I think it's better if I go now and you handle the situation." She yanked her tank top over her head and crossed the room to the refrigerator without looking at him.

Her red-gold hair was a tangled mess around her shoulders, and she had that just fucked look. A shot of possessiveness rolled through him. Damn it, he wanted her to stay. He wasn't done with her. Not even close.

He approached and laid his hands on her shoulders and turned her to face him. "We can make it fast in the shower. I can be efficient, how you like it?"

Her lips twitched. "You're incorrigible. I really don't want the crew to see me skulking out of your room. I've got a chance of making it back now."

Damn if she wasn't right. He didn't want to embarrass

her. He tugged her against him and savored the feel of her. Her arms slid around his neck and she gazed up at him.

He clasped her jaw in one hand and brushed his mouth against hers, savoring her pillowy lips and her sweet taste. She moaned and deepened the kiss, threading her fingers through his hair.

Not helping.

Reluctantly, he lifted his head and brushed his thumb across her full lower lip. "Can I see you tonight?" Damn it. Shit, where had that come from?

He'd had one taste of Kenzie and craved more. That's where it had come from. Certainly not from his thinking brain.

She stepped back, "Austin, I don't know if that's a good idea." She waved an arm between them. "I don't know if this is a good idea, not with all we have to do to make the grand opening happen on time."

He rubbed his jaw. "I don't know either but I––"

Damn it, he didn't want to leave his room all day if he were being honest about it. Not if Kenzie was in it.

"Not now. Let's get through today and figure it out later. I need to get back, okay?" She shoved her hair back from her face.

He huffed out a breath. "Yeah. I––" Why couldn't he seem to shut up and let her go?

She quickly packed up her groceries and strode to the door. With her hand on the doorknob, she paused and turned toward him. "We'll talk later, okay?"

He flopped back onto the soft mattress and stared at the ceiling, his mind racing. What the actual hell was he going to do? He'd kept his relationships, if you could call them that, super casual since his breakup with Chantelle. He'd been careful not to get involved with women he worked with for obvious reasons.

Damn it. The group hadn't been wrong betting on him and Kenzie. Here he was, after spending one night with her, already wanting more. And not just the sex. She was the most fascinating woman he'd ever met. Sure, her external beauty was appealing but her resilience, strength, and her humor lit her up from the inside out. He felt good around her, plain and simple.

Could they see each other and work together without it complicating things too much? Juggle his responsibilities during the day and spend the nights with her. Because right now, keeping things all business between them seemed impossible.

CHAPTER 15

*K*enzie placed the last packing cube into her suitcase, and zipped it shut. It was Friday morning, and she was meeting Austin in the lobby in five minutes to head to the airport. Time to channel her inner peaceful warrior--a few cleansing breaths and she'd be fine.

No more hiding out like she'd been doing since Monday. After their mind-blowing night together, she had panicked and avoided him. Because of the bizarre, 48 hour airport shut down, Austin had been scrambling to manage the renovations and she had been juggling spa business.

She'd needed space to process the emotions ricocheting around her system like a thousand kernels in a vintage movie theater popcorn machine. Not that she'd figured anything out. Nope, no brilliant epiphanies. No insightful realizations at the end of a meditation session.

Maybe going back and listening to his former band's music, especially focusing on the way he either crooned, growled, or screamed the lyrics, hadn't been the smartest choice.

Each song had taken her on an emotional ride with

pounding drums and fierce guitars. She'd sobbed through a heartbreaking ballad that had sat at #1 on numerous charts for an entire year. Yeah, Mr. *I'm just a happy-go-lucky bad boy with my black leather jacket and shiny motorcycle* had a tender heart. A profound well of emotions simmered beneath Austin's façade.

The man was like an artichoke, with each internal layer, he grew sweeter and softer. More appealing. His sensitive troubled soul called to her like flames beckoned to a moth.

So much for her years of yoga and mindfulness training to control her impulses. All it took was Austin Michaels to shake her foundation. To tempt her to run wild and succumb to her impulses. To play instead of work. To be reckless.

Somehow she'd believed starting fresh in the desert would simplify her life but instead, all the clear-cut lines she'd drawn were smudging like sidewalk chalk drawings during an afternoon rain shower.

Priorities. Her primary goal was making The Sanctuary at The Monroe a smashing success and cementing herself as a spa-industry leader. To accomplish it, she needed to be efficient, practical, and one hundred percent focused on business. Until she'd reached that milestone, everything else had to be relegated to the back burner.

Even Austin. Especially Austin.

She lifted the handle and rolled her lime green suitcase out of her room and marched to the lobby. With each step, her resolve deepened.

On the way to the airport, they would have a reasonable conversation like the adults they were and chalk up the most passionate night of her life to simple chemistry. They could work together and be friends, or at least be friendly, but it was one and done. What's a little sexy time between two expert compartmentalizers who didn't want complications?

Austin sauntered into the lobby from the opposite end, all

lean muscles and shaggy dark hair. His lips quirked up into his customary wicked half-smile and her heart jack-hammered against her ribcage. She sucked in a sharp inhale, but with every step, her awareness grew.

A visceral memory of his beautiful mouth on her skin slammed into her. Her palms grew damp. Oh, she was in trouble. She raised one hand in a half-wave.

Ignored the shakiness of said hand. "Hey."

His long legs ate up the space between them until they were toe to toe. Until she could smell a hint of soap on his smooth skin and feel the pull of his magnetism. "Hey yourself. Ready to go?"

His voice was casual, like the other night was simply a fantasy. Hadn't she wanted him to act like nothing had happened so she could play along? For now. So why did a sliver of disappointment whisper through her?

"I think so. I'm just glad the airport is open again."

He chuckled. "Right? Because somehow I doubt you'd want to ride on the back of my bike to L.A. to catch a flight. Our Uber is out front. Let's go."

"Not ever riding that death machine again, sorry." A quick flare of heat hit low in her belly. Yeah, the motorcycle had scared her, but her fear had morphed into excitement.

Cruising on that machine had been foreplay, plain and simple.

They crossed the broad lobby, exited the double doors, and climbed into the small car. Technically safer than the motorcycle, but Austin's proximity endangered her equilibrium.

In the back seat's confined space, Kenzie pressed her hands together in her lap, fighting the urge to stroke the errant strand of hair falling across Austin's forehead. No time to get into the other night. With herculean effort, she confined the conversation to Ryan and Charlie's upcoming nuptials. Thankfully, it was a quick ride to the airport where a sleek charcoal and white jet awaited them in the private airfield area.

When they ascended the stairs into the plane, Kenzie halted in the doorway, drinking in the luxurious interior. "Holy cow."

She'd worked with ultra-wealthy clients for years, but this was next level luxury. A cream leather couch, trimmed in the same charcoal gray as the exterior sat against one side of the plane. Bucket-style chairs and a leather booth framed a rectangular marbled tabletop.

Two more seats toward the back of the plane sat near an open doorway leading to who knew where? A bedroom? Bathroom? Kitchen? Everything was pristine.

Austin placed one hand on her lower back and heat flashed up her spine. She stepped forward, away from the temptation of those long, blunt fingers, her shoes sinking into plush gray carpet.

"Sorry, first time in a private plane and wow. This is your dad's plane?" The rug was so soft it tempted her to roll around and snuggle into it.

"No, he leased it. Planes like this are super expensive."

Austin tossed his bag down in an open bin, completely at ease. The realization hit her––he'd probably flown private all the time with the band. He certainly didn't seem fazed by the decadence.

"Got it." She placed her bag next to his in the compartment. Together they slid into the sleek booth.

A smiling middle-aged redhead appeared with two glasses of champagne. In crystal flutes, no less. Oh yeah, they weren't in commercial travel land any longer.

"Hi Austin and Ms. Banks, I'm Marie and I'm here to ensure your flight is as enjoyable as possible. Your parents will be right back."

"Please call me Kenzie." Kenzie smiled and accepted the chilled glass. "Thank you so much." Today she'd make an exception and enjoy the premium alcohol.

Austin's eyes widened but he didn't comment about her not asking for sparkling water.

He flashed a grin at the flight attendant. "Hi Marie, you're the best. How's your son doing at Stanford?"

Kenzie swung her gaze to Austin. He knew where the flight attendant's son went to college? How often did he travel private?

The woman's cheeks pinkened. "Jayden is doing great, he decided to major in Chemistry. Thank you so much for asking."

Austin grinned up at her. "He reminds me of Ryan-- always top of his class, making the rest of look like slackers."

Marie shook her head. "Oh shush, Jayden worships you, Mr. Famous Rockstar. He and his friends ask about when your next song is coming out and I keep telling him you've got a new venture."

Austin's smile wavered before he pasted it back on. "Yeah, that's right. Hey, I'm starving. Any snacks for the ride?"

"Of course. I've got a cheese and charcuterie board ready. Now buckle up so we can take off and I'll serve it as soon as we're in the air. Enjoy the bubbles." Marie headed toward the rear of the plane.

Once she was out of hearing distance, Kenzie couldn't resist. "Okay, spill it. Just how often do you fly private? You obviously know Marie if you're asking about her son?"

Austin stared out the window, which was more picture window, less standard porthole style like on commercial jets. His jaw was tight, his chiseled mouth a tight line.

"This is the same company my band used for domestic travel and Marie's been with them for years. I met Jayden a few times and he was a fan of the band. That's all."

Funny how he downplayed his big heart and his kindness to others. He remembered names. He went out of his way to make people smile, to make them feel seen.

He made her feel like he truly saw her. Damn it, why couldn't he just be a cocky ex-rockstar with a chip on his shoulder? He was difficult to resist.

"I think you're sweet."

He snapped his gaze toward her, his dark eyebrows up to his hairline. "Sweet?"

She settled back into the buttery leather and sipped the excellent champagne. "Yes, sweet and considerate. Taking a moment to ask about her son. Lending me your car so I didn't have to go through the hassle of the rental car. Most employers don't bother."

"I like people, that's all." Then he leaned forward in his seat, his midnight blue eyes blazing. "And if you think I see you as just my employee, especially after being inside you, you're out of your mind."

Kenzie choked on the champagne she'd just sipped and started coughing as the bubbles tickled her nostrils.

Austin sprang from his chair and massaged her back. Not helpful. Not helpful at all. She held up the hand with her glass and he plucked it out while she continued to hack up a lung.

Marie hurried out with a glass of water. "Here hon, sip this water. It will help. That champagne is so dry, you aren't the first one to have it go down the wrong pipe."

With a grateful glance, Kenzie accepted the glass and chugged half of it. At least the woman didn't know the real reason she was gasping and choking. Austin's words enflamed her entire being, like taking a match to a powder keg.

Angela and Chris appeared and joined them across the

table. "Oh great, you two are already settled in. Are you okay, Kenzie?" Angela said.

Oh my god, what if they'd heard Austin? Heat rose in her cheeks.

Once she'd settled down, the pilot reminded them over the speaker that they were taking off and to check their seat belts. Kenzie fussed with the buckle and kept her gaze down as long as possible. It wasn't often she was at a loss for words but right now? All she could think about was Austin and their passionate night.

"Before we start on the madness of the weekend, catch me up on the hotel since we last spoke. Ryan told us you're doing a great job. On track for opening day in September?" Chris asked.

Austin's shoulders tensed. "Yeah, the renovations are on schedule. We've got a great local crew. Lucas is doing a lot of the financials."

Angela placed her hand over his. "We are so proud of you, Austin. Ryan's the only one with hotel experience and all you boys are knocking it out of the park. Each of you contributes something unique and your Food and Beverage knowledge is an asset, just like Lucas' love of numbers benefits the team. Let him take the brunt of them until you have a local accountant on board."

"Yeah, I am. Lucas has interviews set up for when he comes out next month."

"You know my philosophy on successful ventures: surround yourself with people who are experts in their fields and do what you do best." Chris raised his glass. "Cheers."

Angela beamed. "Here's to Hotel Kings' continued success."

A hint of sadness tugged at Kenzie's heart. Not that she would begrudge anybody else a loving family but observing first-hand the love and respect between them tasted bittersweet. She'd never experienced it with her parents. Keeping the discussion on the hotel was the safest bet.

"I'm thrilled to be a small part of it." Her gaze swept all three of them, her lips curved upward.

Angela laid one hand on Chris's sleeve. "We've found it fascinating to see it all unfold and how each hotel has a unique flair that seems to suit everyone. Like the environmental restoration at Maison du Soleil in Paso Robles, and the restored dairy farm of Cypress Coast Ranch. We were surprised Austin chose Palm Springs, but I think The Monroe will be a perfect fit."

"We did think you'd end up back in L.A. but I'm glad you're here instead," Chris said.

Kenzie tilted her head. "I know I'm new around here, but I can't picture Austin in Beverly Hills." Like, at all.

"Yeah, that's Lucas and his designer suits, not me. I told you both I'm done with the L.A. life." Austin's knuckles were white where he gripped his denim clad thigh.

Kenzie shrugged, feeling the tension in the air, eager to diffuse it. "We're both adjusting to the desert. It's definitely a change of pace. So how did the movie location scout go?"

Chris grinned and nodded. "It's perfect. We'll be able to use some streets in downtown Palm Springs––permits willing––and the high desert is authentic. It's not far from the Marine Base in 29 Palms."

"That's great, Chris. When are you planning to start shooting?" Austin said.

"Oh, it's not on the schedule until next January. When it is nice and cool around here." Chris fanned a hand in front of his face. "How are you two holding up with the heat?"

"Air-conditioning and the pool." Kenzie laughed.

"The pool and the a/c," Austin said at the same time.

Angela looked between them, her dark eyes searching. "Well, that pool does look very inviting. Austin's always loved the water so I'm assuming you two have that in common?"

"Swimming has always been a great complement to my yoga practice. But for now, it's just the coolest place around. I'll probably be sitting in the pool working on my laptop."

"Sounds like a plan. So have you gotten my son to practice yoga with you yet?" Angela asked.

"Funny you should mention it. I told him he should join me for some private yoga sessions in the mornings. For both the personal benefits and the professional ones of really understanding the offerings at the spa and studio."

"Can we watch? Maybe film him for a promotional clip?" Chris's eyes gleamed with mischief and a dimple creased his cheek.

Austin held up both hands. "Hey, everyone just calm down. Kenzie is the online yoga star, not me. And I'm planning on joining her, I just don't want anything to slip through the cracks. I need to stay focused."

"Yoga helps you focus. Tons of athletes and CEOs use it as a tool to get mental clarity and be more productive." Kenzie's gaze honed in on him.

"I know, but--"

Chris spoke up. "That's a great point. Heck, I need that."

"I've told you both a million times." Angela's lips twitched. "I love yoga and agree with you, Kenzie."

"I said I was going to do it. Kenzie's only been on site for a few weeks. We'll get to it," Austin said.

Chris rubbed his jaw. "Actually, this gives me an idea. I think yoga on set would be amazing for the actors and crew. Do you teach all kinds of groups?"

"I've taught across the gamut. Fancy studios, gyms, corporate yoga, yoga for seniors, and yoga for cancer recovery. I also used to teach for a company that managed elite triathlons around the country. If people training for an Ironman can find some time for yoga, anybody can."

"Well, what do you think about me bringing you out to teach on set?" Chris said.

Her throat tightened. "Wow, I'd be honored and I'm sure I can work it into the schedule. That will be four months after opening, so my schedule should be regulated. Thank you so much for offering."

Austin's dad was proposing such an amazing opportunity after spending a grand total of thirty minutes with her? Other people's parents routinely helped their kids, but her own dad barely acknowledged her existence, much less took care of her. She'd worked her butt off for everything she had, and nobody simply offered to make her life easier like this.

Just like Austin's consideration and subtle gestures made her feel seen, his parents' easy acceptance helped her feel like she belonged. Like they had faith in her abilities without her having to prove a thing. And Charlie and Ryan certainly hadn't been obliged to include her in the wedding festivities. Everyone had welcomed her into the Hotel Kings family.

A wave of emotion threatened to overwhelm her-- coming to The Monroe was the right choice. She'd dreamt of finding a true home but couldn't have envisioned how quickly it had fallen into place.

Before she blurted out something embarrassing, Marie materialized with an incredible charcuterie board, gleaming with gorgeous fruits, plump cheeses, toasted nuts, and delicate slivers of prosciutto and salami. Chris turned to Angela, and they fell into a discussion about something movie related.

"You okay now? I think we should discuss a few things once we land in Monterey. And I'd like to go first." Austin's raspy voice had a thread of command within and damned if that wasn't sexy.

Since she was still struggling for composure, she kept her gaze on the food and nodded.

"Kenzie, look at me."

She lifted her gaze to his sincere one and her heart took a long tumbling roll in her chest. Crap was she in trouble. "That's fine. But for now, let's keep it straightforward."

"Austin, sweetie, come look at a few things I got for Ryan and Charlie. I want to show them to you before we land." Angela stood, tall and long-limbed like her son.

He rose and joined his mom at the back of the plane. Seeing their obvious closeness warmed her heart. If anything, seeing Austin with his parents made him even more attractive. His mom and stepdad obviously loved and were intensely proud of their son.

But time to steer her attention away from Austin Michaels' irresistibleness. She leaned forward and asked Chris a question about his upcoming film. One she might actually get to work on.

Focus on career. Not on wanting Austin.

CHAPTER 16

*A*ngela and Kenzie preceded Austin off the plane. The Monterey breeze lifted her irresistible scent to his nostrils. Of course, now he knew she not only smelled like his favorite fruit, but tasted like peaches, too.

Dangerous. And now he'd learned her sweetness went so much deeper than the surface. That her beauty wasn't in the perfection of her features, but in her brave sensitive soul. How he was going to act cool around her this weekend was a freakin' mystery.

He was so screwed.

"Hey guys, over here," Lucas shouted.

His brother, Grant, and Lucas waved them over to an enormous silver SUV with the Cypress Coast Ranch logo emblazoned on the passenger door. One of the many perks of flying private was literally exiting onto the tarmac and strolling straight to your ride.

They strode to the vehicle, stored the luggage, and hopped inside. Chris joined Lucas up front, Grant and their mom took the middle row, leaving the rear for him and Kenzie.

Because of course he couldn't get a break.

Because being in the back seat together meant he would be close enough to touch her warm skin. Be enveloped in her delicious scent. Could he hold his breath all the way to the resort?

Kenzie scooted close to the window, creating a sliver of space between them. But he couldn't ignore the way the sunlight glimmered off her shiny hair and highlighted the curve of her cheek.

The urge to drag her onto his lap and capture her plump pink lips surged through him and he gripped the edge of the leather seat. Austin adjusted his now too-tight pants. *Damn.*

Now he knew how responsive she was to his touch, how she murmured and purred, and how she cried his name when she came apart in his arms. Dangerous? More like life-threatening. How long was this ride going to take?

Grant angled back in his seat. "How's everything? Any news on your car, Kenzie?"

"The police think it's a lost cause but they're making me wait a few weeks before they'll let me claim it on my insurance." She shook her head, her high ponytail swinging.

Austin gripped the edges of the seat and silently recited baseball statistics. All he wanted was to wrap her long hair around his fist, tug her head back, and lick her long slender neck like an ice cream cone.

Seemingly oblivious to his agony, she continued in her throaty voice. "Austin has been sweet enough to lend me his car, so it's been fine."

"That's my boy." His mom smiled at him and shifted her gaze to Kenzie. "We also have a few extra cars out at the ranch, so if you need your own wheels, we're happy to help. And I am sorry it happened. How did you get back to Palm Springs last weekend?"

Kenzie's eyes widened. "That's so generous of you,

Angela. Wow." She cleared her throat. "Well, I rode on the back of your son's motorcycle. My first and last time."

"We made it home safe, right?" Although every moment with her perfect body flush against his back had been exquisite torture.

Kenzie's delicate nostrils flared, then she smiled at his mom and brother. "We did. So, is there anything I can do this afternoon to help?"

"That's so sweet of you to offer but between Charlie and Lucy, this weekend is already a precise military operation. All we need to do is relax. It's going to be gorgeous," Angela said.

The conversation drifted between details of the weekend's festivities and general small talk, and he was able to wrangle his body under control. For now, anyway. Finally, the car entered Cypress Coast Ranch's wide open gates, framed by trees and buckets of flowers.

When they parked and exited the car, Kenzie pressed a slender hand to her chest, her eyes wide. "This is the most beautiful place I've ever seen."

His gaze lingered on her profile another moment––the most beautiful thing he'd ever seen. "And planes can always land here." Time to rely on his strongest defense mechanism––humor.

She laughed and turned toward him. "Some people have all the luck."

Lucy hurried to greet them, a clipboard in her hand. "You all made it on time. Now, I've got schedules and room assignments for everyone. The rehearsal is at 4 on the beach followed immediately by drinks and dinner in the gardens so we can catch the sunset."

"As long as mine is color-coded and tabbed, we're good." Austin winked at the petite powerhouse who owned his friend Cameron's heart.

"Sarcasm gets you everything here. Now be good." Lucy wagged a finger at him.

Chris slung an arm around his shoulders. "Oh, he'll be good. Where do you have us?"

"You and Angela are with the Taylors in the cottage closest to the restaurant." Lucy handed Chris an envelope. "Austin, you and Lucas are in the same building with Jack and Campbell. And Kenzie, you're with Brigitte in the cottage closest to the beach. Any questions?"

When nobody responded, Lucy beamed. "Settle in and feel free to explore. It's just family here today. And everyone at the beach at 4 pm sharp. Kenzie feel free to join us or just meet for the reception. Up to you."

"Thanks so much Lucy. I've got a few calls to make, so I'll head down now and see you all later." Kenzie accepted her envelope and sauntered off.

Austin watched the sway of her hips and the bounce of that tempting ponytail until she disappeared down the lane. Something tugged in his chest.

"Earth to Austin. Hellooo..." Lucy snapped her fingers in front of his face.

He refocused. Everyone was staring at him. Lucas smirked, and Chris and his mom were studying him like he was the newest exhibit at the zoo.

"What? I'm ready for my orders. Reporting for duty." He saluted Lucy.

"You like her, don't you, sweetie?" His mom smiled. "We like her too. She fits in so well with everyone."

Damn, his mom missed nothing. Now that her first two sons were happily paired up, her hawk eye had been focused on him. He'd never been able to hide his feelings from her.

But Kenzie didn't want a relationship. Wasn't there some famous quote about when someone told you something to believe them? If they hooked up a few times, it was their business. She could handle it. So could he.

Sure, he was catching feelings for Kenzie, but he had it under control. All he had to do was continue reminding himself that everything was temporary. Losing his dad and Tommy, walking away from his dream career with Black Velvet Machine, and starting over made that clear.

He was already playing catch up with the other guys with his lack of education and business training. No way would he fail his brother--not when Ryan had taken a chance on him.

"She's great. And yes, I think she's gorgeous. But she's my employee and we're becoming friends, that's all." And did his nose just grow eight inches? Maybe ten?

Lucas snorted and arched a ginger eyebrow. "Because that worked out so well for Ryan and Jack and Cam?"

Chris laughed and pointed a finger at Lucas. "I was thinking the same thing. So that means you're next, right Lucas? Isn't Brigitte going to be the new concierge at the Beverly Hills hotel?"

Lucas' mouth snapped shut and he pushed his glasses back onto the bridge of his nose. Austin's shoulders relaxed; thank god his stepdad was great at directing not just movies but conversations.

Lucy clapped her hands. "Boys, follow me. The other guys are waiting for you. Things to do before the rehearsal. Angela and Chris, you've got a nice bottle of Chablis chilling in your room. See you at the beach." She trotted away, leaving them to follow.

Lucas elbowed him and whispered, "Hey, I didn't want to bring this up in front of everyone, but have you signed off on those employee financials yet?"

His gut tightened. "Sorry, this week has been nuts because of the airport closure. Do you need them now or is it okay if I finish up Sunday when I'm back in Palm Springs?"

"I needed them today but if you get them to me by Sunday night, I'll make it work."

"Yeah, me and Kenzie are taking the plane back early on Sunday, so I'll get them to you by the afternoon." No need to admit he hadn't forgotten because of the shutdown but because he'd been thinking about Kenzie. Time to remember The Monroe came first.

"So, Austin, will I be seeing you down at my cottage later?" Brigitte gazed at him with a sly grin.

"Why, is that where the after-party is?"

They walked up to the gardens from the beach. Ryan and Charlie's rehearsal had gone off without a hitch. The officiant was a sweet older lady with a soothing voice and a wide smile. Fortunately, his brother and his fiancée had crafted their own vows and kept them short and sweet. Jack was best man, so all Austin and the other guys had to do was escort the bridesmaids. Easy.

"Well, I am rooming with Kenzie so I thought you two might want some private time." Brigitte waggled her eyebrows.

His step hitched. "Seriously?" What the actual hell? Had Kenzie confided in her?

"I saw that Hollywood kiss last weekend. You two can't keep your eyes off each other. I assumed you'd, how do you Americans call it? Hook up?"

"I'm here to celebrate my brother and your best friend. That's enough romance for me." He forced a chuckle.

"Et voila." she waved a hand. "I said hook up and you jumped straight to romance. You do like her. I'm always right about these things."

"Yes, she's clairvoyant." Charlie stepped up and wrapped

an arm around each of them. "She called me out over your big brother when I swore up and down I couldn't stand him. I'm totally winning the bet."

"Did anyone actually bet against us hooking up? How's that going to work at payout time? You give us the money?" He maintained an impassive expression––these two couldn't suspect his and Kenzie's secret.

Whatever was happening with Kenzie was between them and only them. He wouldn't betray her confidence and that meant not admitting to their hook up unless she permitted it.

A crease appeared on Charlie's brow. "I don't think so. Huh, I guess we didn't think that through. I'll ask Lucas, he's the numbers guy."

They reached the opening in the split-rail fence leading into the hotel's lush gardens. A few round tables were set up for the group dinner tonight, lemon yellow tablecloths fluttering in the wind. Strands of twinkling lights adorned the trees, standing out against the greenery like stars in a summer sky. A formal bar sat under the awning next to the ballroom entrance. Thank god.

"Oooh, your accountant is at the bar flirting with Kenzie. Are you jealous?" Brigitte's eyes narrowed.

"You ladies have too much time on your hands. Let's grab a drink." And why was Lucas looming over Kenzie?

A stab of possessiveness hit him, and his stride turned purposeful. What were they discussing that had her face glowing?

She wore one of those flowy long dresses with skinny straps that emphasized her sculpted yoga arms. Her red-gold hair cascaded around her shoulders in a silky curtain, reminding him of how it looked spread on the pillow next to him. He ground his molars together and exhaled a deep breath.

Time to remember they were co-workers at his brother's

wedding with his entire freaking family. Not lovers. Not a couple. Tonight, he'd hang with his brothers and Kenzie could spend time bonding with everyone. So why was his heart hammering against his ribs when he greeted her?

Lucas pointed at him and skirted around the bar. "Perfect timing. Can you man the bar for a minute? The staff won't start for another half an hour. I've got a quick fire to put out for Ryan." Without waiting for a response, he headed toward the lobby building.

"Bubbles for us, please. And where did my husband to be disappear to?" Charlie surveyed the scene.

"My mom took him somewhere for a chat. He'll be right back. And then you'll have him forever, so it's all good, right?"

Charlie beamed at him. "Yes I will."

Comfortable behind the bar, because hey, that's the only other job he'd had besides the band, he poured and handed flutes of champagne to Charlie and Brigitte.

"I'd love a glass too, please," Kenzie said.

His mouth dropped open. "You want another glass of champagne?" He hadn't mentioned it on the plane in front of his parents, but this was unexpected.

"Surprise." She shrugged one sculpted shoulder.

Brigitte laughed. "I like your style. And they call me fancy."

"Austin knows I don't usually drink alcohol. But I do indulge in the occasional glass of bubbles for celebrations."

"Oh gosh, you must think we're a bunch of winos after last weekend." Charlie's dark eyes widened. "Is it because of your yoga lifestyle?"

Kenzie's smile wavered. "Just a personal choice, not a big deal. No, I don't think you're winos."

"One glass of bubbly coming up." He handed her a full flute.

Their fingers brushed, and heat zipped up his arm. The icy liquid spilled but failed to cool him off. It would take a freakin' firehose to subdue the blaze this woman ignited in him.

Pull it together or Charlie would figure out he was into Kenzie. He contemplated the array of liquor bottles. Champagne or beer wasn't going to cut it tonight--he needed whiskey.

Usually when his emotions jumbled in his chest like this, he released them through his music. Over the last few years, he'd kept his interactions casual, more surface--safer that way. But Kenzie stirred him up and without his creative outlet to purge the mix of feelings, he was a powder keg. Alcohol wasn't the answer, but some whiskey was his best bet tonight.

Ryan and their mom stood in the open sliding doors to the ballroom, deep in conversation. Mr. and Mrs. Taylor, Cameron and Campbell's parents, joined them.

"You've got to meet the Taylors, they are fabulous." Charlie linked her arm through Kenzie's and Brigitte's and started walking toward them. "Thanks for the drinks, Austin."

Kenzie looked back, her gaze finding his, her aquamarine eyes guarded. She turned before he could react. And what would his reaction even look like? Yeah, he'd file these emotions away to consider later. Much later. He downed his whiskey and poured two more fingers.

"Service, bartender." Jack and Campbell appeared at the bar, and Jack tapped his fist against it a few times. "Me and my woman are thirsty."

"Do you see what I have to put up with here? Can you pour me some champagne and *my man* will have what you're having, right?" Campbell smirked.

Jack leaned down and pressed a kiss to his fiancée's cheek and she beamed up at him. Last Fall, they'd had to share an apartment during harvest season while opening Maison du Soleil in Paso Robles. Turned out Campbell had crushed on her brother Cam's best friend since high school and the rest was history.

Austin's lips twitched. "Whiskey neat. You two look like those ex-supermodel actors starring in a Hallmark movie. Too good-looking to be real." But the attorney and Master Sommelier were two of his closest friends and as genuine as they came.

"Yeah, my man is hot. But look around, this group looks like the cast of a soap opera wedding. Including your Kenzie." Campbell winked.

Austin closed his eyes for a moment and counted to five. "She is not my Kenzie. Soap opera wedding is right but just because Lucas, me, and Jon are still single doesn't mean you need play matchmaker. Remember she works for me."

"As the LLCs attorney, I'll offer a friendly reminder that we don't have a no-fraternization policy." Jack's green eyes gleamed with humor.

"Yeah, yeah." Austin's phone buzzed and he fished it out of his back pocket. He frowned and shook his head.

Why was Liam texting him again––what part of a hint could the Brit not catch? How much clearer could he be that he wasn't returning to the band? He tucked his phone away without reading the unwanted message.

"Everything cool?" Jack asked.

"Yeah, just a lot going on with the opening. You know what I mean." He hadn't confided in any of his friends about Liam's pressuring him. No point.

Jack's dark brows drew together. "If you need some help, I can carve out some time."

"Me too. I've already curated the initial wine lists for Fall and Winter. But maybe we can fly down and give you a hand? Double date with you and Kenzie?" Campbell smirked.

He pointed at Campbell. "Stop. I've got it handled. Ryan and Jon are already coming out. Lucas too."

His phone buzzed again. It was Liam again——time to text him and make it crystal clear the past was staying in the past. Then he'd block his number.

No regrets. He refused to dwell on the past. He was officially an ex lead singer who ran a luxury hotel. And he'd play acoustically for special occasions. Like his brother's wedding. Case closed.

His mom waved, beckoning them over. "Okay, everyone can pour their own drinks until the servers arrive. Let's go join the parents. No more work talk this weekend."

"Excellent point." Campbell mimicked sealing her lips and tossing away the key.

Time to focus on enjoying his brother's rehearsal dinner. Although keeping his distance from Kenzie would test his self-control. But they were two mature adults, not two teenagers who couldn't keep their hands off each other. Right?

CHAPTER 17

The trouble started at the reception, after the breathtaking wedding ceremony. Charlie and Ryan took their vows barefoot, toes in the soft sugar white sand, beneath a simple arch adorned with fluttering lavender ribbons. An intimate group watched from elegant chairs facing the gorgeous Pacific ocean, cypress trees, and the natural beauty of Monterey. The newlyweds strolled down the aisle hand in hand with the sun setting over the midnight blue water. While the wedding party, including Austin, were photographed, Kenzie and the rest of the guests enjoyed the cocktail reception.

An incredible dinner had taken place in the garden where guests were seated at round tables adorned with lavender tablecloths and enormous vases of powder blue and cream hydrangeas, along with gorgeous cream china place settings. She'd sat next to Austin and her self-control evaporated.

Between the proximity to his frequent laughter, the heat from his skin, and the clean beachy scent of his ebony hair, she'd struggled not to pounce the moment he sat down. Stolen glances, brushes of their hands, and flirty banter escalated. And that's what had them sneaking to the empty hotel room and tearing into each other.

Kenzie tugged Austin's midnight blue linen shirt out from his dark slacks, her hands impatient, breath unsteady. She stroked her hands up his smooth skin, over those tempting carved V-shaped grooves, along the lean muscle of his six-pack, to his strong, square pecs. Like the finest silk covering the hardest steel.

His dark head dropped back. "Kenzie," he rasped. "You're killing me."

Power surged through her veins. The knowledge she drove him wild stoked her own arousal even more. She wound her arms around his neck and leaned into him. "Kiss me."

He captured her mouth, then reached down and cupped her through the thin fabric of her sundress. Her vision blurred when he shoved the skirt up around her waist, then stroked along her seam.

"Fuck, you're so wet. So ready for me." His head dropped to her shoulder, and he nipped at her neck, sending lightning strikes straight to her already molten core.

"Mmmm…" She tugged his head up and kissed him, savoring his warm, sweet breath.

He continued stroking against her gossamer thin thong and tugged the fabric aside. He spread her apart and drove two fingers inside of her. When his thumb circled her center, she cried against his lips, pleasure rushing through her.

"Yes, oh yes, that's it, baby." He added another finger, increasing his pace. She was teetering on the edge, her legs trembling, her fingers gripping his broad shoulders, as she rocked against his hand, desperate for release. Waves of sensation pulsated through her, she was so close. Her eyes drifted shut.

"Open your eyes. I want you looking at me when you come," He demanded, his voice urgent.

She obeyed and was rewarded by the feral gleam in his deep blue eyes. "Now. Come for me now."

He pressed the heel of his hand against her center. Instantly, she shattered into a million pieces, her back bowing away from the wall. He growled and slid one hand up to pinch her taut nipple, aftershocks vibrating through her entire system. He captured her mouth, and murmured, "I need to be inside you. Now."

"Yes. Tell me you have a condom." She slid her hands down his sleekly muscled back and grasped his perfect ass.

"Wallet. Back pocket."

She yanked out the wallet while he unfastened his belt and shoved his pants down, freeing himself. Then in one swift move, he tore her thong off and tossed it behind him. Goosebumps rose along her skin, and anticipation rendered her mouth dry.

Her fingers shook as she tore open the packet and together they sheathed his rock hard erection. He slid a hand under one thigh and lifted it, opening her wide. With one powerful thrust, he drove himself deep, pinning her against the smooth hard wall.

They both groaned and he held still, giving her a moment to get used to him.

"Austin." Desperation surged through her. She stroked her fingernails through his hair and tugged--impatient now.

"You feel so fucking good, Kenzie." He started taking her in long, deliberate strokes. With the wall behind her and him holding her immobile, all she could do was urge him on.

Deeper. Harder. Closer. He was kissing her now, his mouth slanted over hers, his tongue stroking against hers, his hips pounding into her. In the silence of the empty guest room, the sound of their flesh slapping, the slickness of their skin, and the scent of his shampoo surrounded her. Tension escalated and she rocked against him, the pressure just where she needed it.

"Come for me baby. Give me another one." He rasped, never stopping kissing her, never stopping his relentless rhythm.

"Oh my god, yes." A constellation of lights burst behind her eyelids, and her orgasm slammed through her like a lightning strike.

With her name on his lips, he groaned, and followed her over the edge. He dropped his forehead to hers, their breath mingling, his body heavy against hers.

"I need my leg back. Cramp." She hissed at the sharp pain.

"I thought yoga teachers could hold poses forever?" He pulled out, then released her leg.

She laughed and massaged her hamstring. "Like you would know, Mr. Avoids Yoga."

He smoothed her hair back from her face. "I thought this was my private yoga session? Tantra, right?"

"You're too much." She giggled and studied his eyes gleaming with satisfaction, his relaxed expression. His ability to swing from passion to humor so effortlessly was one more quality she loved about him.

Her heart jolted and her breath lodged in her throat. *Loved?* No, no, no, she couldn't be in love with Austin Michaels. It wasn't in her well-detailed life plan. Panic skittered down her spine. It was too soon, she'd only known him for weeks––you can't fall in love in weeks.

And here she was, sneaking off with him to have sex during his brother's, their boss's, wedding reception.

She stiffened, suddenly needing to get some space and regain her composure.

"Kenzie?" Austin's retreated a step, his dark brows lifted. "You okay?"

"It just hit me that it's the middle of Ryan and Charlie's reception and we need to get back. You've got to play, and we can't miss the cake cutting. I need to clean up." Nor could anyone discover they'd disappeared together. Not exactly her most professional move.

She tugged her dress down and smoothed the silky fabric. And spotted her torn thong on the floor. Heat flooded her cheeks––because the moment he'd ripped it off her had been scorching. She bent down, grabbed the ruined fabric, and hurried to the restroom.

"I'll just be a second." She called over her shoulder, noting that he'd adjusted his shirt and zipped up his pants, looking disheveled and heartbreakingly sexy.

He kept his gaze down, crossing the room toward the trash can. "Take your time."

She closed the door behind her with a quiet click and assessed the damage in the mirror. Holy hell, her lips were swollen and red, her hair was mussed, and her mascara was more on her cheeks than her lashes. Yeah, no mistaking what she'd been doing. She closed her eyes for a moment and pressed shaky hands to her belly.

Her mother would cackle with glee and tell her she was just like her father. That she'd inherited his reckless streak. And no matter how rigid and organized she was, no matter how much yoga she practiced, no matter if she didn't touch a drink, she'd never escape her genes.

Both her parents were alcoholics who only cared about themselves. Her dad functioned at work, but off the clock? He'd gotten DUIs, created mortifying scenes with drunken tirades in front of neighbors, and generally been an asshole at home.

She'd spent most of her childhood taking care of them, instead of the other way around.

Sure, they had provided food and shelter and material

things, but they'd never supported her emotionally. Never praised her for getting good grades or attended any of her dance recitals. Never told her she was loved.

A wave of nausea rolled through her. Time to eradicate her narcissistic mother's spiteful voice whispering in her brain. Time to make a plan. She wouldn't panic. She'd freshen up, they'd return to the reception, and she'd force herself to mingle. Thank god dinner was over so nobody would notice if they weren't sitting next to each other.

She didn't trust herself around him, her usual ability to file away her emotions seemingly evaporated. The layers of self-control and composure she'd painstakingly constructed over the years were in tatters. All it took was one sexy, tortured, beautiful ex-rockstar and she'd ridden a motorcycle, had sex with him more than once—all in a matter of weeks. If that wasn't reckless, what was?

Because now she was falling for him for real and it was impossible. Too messy. Too complicated.

Too prone to derail her plan to cement her career and new home before even considering looking for her life partner.

She repaired her make-up and combed her hair into a semblance of order. Thank god the typical Monterey breeze in Cypress Coast Ranch's lush ocean view gardens tousled everyone's hair.

She practiced five rounds of extended exhale breathing, desperate to soothe her nervous system and get her hummingbird heart rate under control. Time to act like the confident, calm yoga teacher Hotel Kings had hired. As opposed to the wild woman who'd just had sex against a wall with her dress around her waist. She smoothed her hair back one more time and opened the door.

Austin sat on the edge of the bed, looking at his phone. He glanced up, his expression unreadable. "Are you ready?

It's about time for me to play the song for their first dance before the band starts."

"Oh god, do you think they're looking for you? Noticed we're gone? Everyone was mingling after dinner, right? Do you think we should enter separately?" Her fingers tightened to a death grip on her purse—it was a wonder the fabric didn't disintegrate beneath her hands.

It wasn't like he'd convinced her to sneak off with him. But she had to create some distance now or she'd crumble. The jumble of emotions simmering beneath the surface threatened to overwhelm her.

His eyes shuttered. "Yeah, nobody knows about us. Why don't I go get my guitar, and you come out in a few minutes."

The silence hung heavy in the air. Awkward. Mere minutes ago, he had been inside her, and now they were polite strangers. She didn't know how to bridge the gap.

She managed a nod. "Okay. Sounds good."

With one more lingering look, he turned and left the suite. Her shoulders sagged and she sank onto the edge of the bed. Time to pull on her big girl panties—figuratively of course since her own underwear was a torn fragment stuffed into her purse—and join the party.

Back to reality. She rose, turned off the lights, and left the suite. When she reached the reception, the guests were gathered in the awning-covered patio area where Charlie and Ryan began cutting the three tiered, exquisite wedding cake. She slipped into the crowd and cheered from a distance before she returned to the table.

Austin wasn't there but Brigitte sat with Dylan, Sam, and Amanda and their husbands and waved her into the seat next to them.

"I'm so proud of those two for not smashing cake into each other's faces. They had to follow Holt and my lead and be civilized." Sam grinned.

Holt barked out a laugh. "Yeah, we set the example."

Just inside the ballroom on a small dais, Austin chatted with the musicians in the three piece band, who smacked him on the back and wandered off.

He sat on the stool, fiddled with his guitar, then adjusted the microphone. His dark hair fell across his brow and his sooty eyelashes rested on the top of his cheekbones. He was heartbreakingly handsome.

He leaned in and addressed the guests. "Hi everyone, For the first dance, I've got a special song for my big brother and his beautiful bride. It's called *Beautiful You*. So clear the dance floor and make way for Ryan and Charlie."

Guests clapped as the newlyweds entered the small dance floor. Ryan pulled Charlie close, and she wound her arms around his neck. Bliss radiated off the golden-haired couple, who were lost in each other's eyes.

The moment Austin strummed the opening chord, the room grew silent, then his haunting, husky voice filled the high-ceilinged room. Goosebumps rose along every inch of her skin. He sang of gazes locking, hearts longing, once in a lifetime chances. With each gorgeous word, a magnetic pull drew her to him. The party, the reception dropped away.

Out of her peripheral vision, the happy couple twirled slowly on the dance floor, like something out of a dream. But all she could see was Austin. His eyes had been half-closed for the beginning of the song but then his indigo gaze caught hers, emotion shining in their depths. Her breath hitched and she clasped her hands together, unable to look away. Unable to sever their connection.

For the rest of the love ballad, an invisible thread bound them across the space. An unbreakable gossamer strand between Austin and her. Her pulse thundered through her veins. He closed the song on a long hopeful note and after a few seconds of silence, the room erupted into applause.

Yeah, he might not be a rockstar anymore, but he was without a doubt one of the most talented, heartfelt singers she'd ever heard. And judging from the reactions around her, that anyone had ever heard. His lips curved into a half-smile, not his usual mischievous grin. "Charlie and Ryan, everyone."

Austin rose but before he could move, Ryan strode across the room and caught him in a bear hug. For a few moments, they held each other tight before Ryan thumped him on the back and raised one of Austin's arms aloft.

"*The* Austin Michaels, everyone. My baby brother is one talented guy. The best. Before the band and dancing starts, Charlie's tossing the bouquet. So, all the single people, get on up here."

Jon materialized next to her and Brigitte. "Come on, single ladies, let's do this. But fair warning, I'll fight you for those flowers. I'm ready for Mr. Right."

"Oh, I don't want that bouquet. It's all yours." Kenzie gripped her champagne flute. No way was she participating in the archaic tradition. Even though she didn't believe whoever caught the flowers would get married next, no need to tempt fate.

Brigitte shook her head. "I'm never getting married. You two go."

"Don't ruin the fun. Come on." Jon corralled them onto the dance floor with the rest of the married couples cheering them on.

Without making a scene, she couldn't evade the ritual, but nothing could force her to catch the prize. She pasted a smile on her face when Charlie stepped onto the platform with the admittedly gorgeous bouquet and peeked over her shoulder.

Jon waved his arms. "Right here, throw it here, boss!"

Charlie winked, faced away from the crowd, and complied.

Both she and Brigitte stood motionless, like two marble

statues. Jon jumped in the air, his fingers grasping for the wedding flowers. His hand closed around the stems but then somehow the bouquet slapped against her chest. Her reflexes kicked in and that's how she ended up with a bouquet of lavender, blue, and white blooms in her hands.

"Oh girl, you're next, whether you like it or not." Jon smirked.

She thrust the bouquet at him. "You take it. You said you've got someone in mind. I don't want them."

"You can't give them away––you caught them, Kenzie. Besides they're gorgeous and smell delicious. They'll make our suite smell fantastic. And here comes Angela." Brigitte sniffed the fragrant blossoms.

Kenzie nibbled on the inside of her cheek. No time to make a scene when Austin's mom approached. She twirled in a circle and held the flowers aloft, as if she was excited.

"Charlie's not the only one who's happy you caught the bouquet," Angela said, a wide smile on her lovely face.

Kenzie's breath lodged in her throat and words eluded her. Austin's mom was excited she'd caught the wedding flowers? "I, uh…"

"Nobody can miss the way you and my son look at each other. Tonight's the first time I've heard my son sing in a very long time and I have a feeling it might be your influ-ence," Angela said.

Kenzie exhaled a shaky breath. "Thank you Angela. I don't know what to say––" Shock battled with joy in her chest. This incredible woman barely knew her but could be so kind and warm?

A lively song started up and people entered the dance floor, ready for the revelry to continue. Brigitte and Jon joined the other guests.

"No need to say anything, sweetie. We think you're fabulous. No pressure. Now I'm off to grab my husband and dance." She winked and sauntered away.

Kenzie pressed her hands to her belly, where a kaleidoscope of butterflies flapped their wings. Austin's mom was the polar opposite of her own––all easy affection and acceptance.

The short hairs on the back of her neck prickled and she searched the room for the source.

Austin stood near the open doorway, watching her, his jaw tight. Then his expression relaxed into one of his devil-may-care grins. Without a word, he turned and disappeared into the evening.

Yeah, Austin's song had been for the newlyweds but the way he'd looked at her while he sang it?

As if he meant the words for her and her alone.

As if she wasn't the only one catching feelings.

As if their relationship wasn't only physical.

And what was she going to do about that now?

ustin reclined against the cushy leather seat and watched Kenzie across the jet's center table. With laser precision, she lined up multi-colored pens and two notebooks next to her laptop. The stark contrast of her controlled movements to her unrestrained response in the hotel room last night flashed through him.

So proper and meticulous today. So wild and uninhibited yesterday. The distinct facets of her personality fascinated him. And were freakin' adorable. *Mine.* A stab of possessiveness struck him.

Yeah, he was in trouble. After the weekend seeing how happy all his couple friends were, something inside him had shifted. Kenzie was special. Talented, resilient, passionate, and so damn beautiful. If Ryan, Jack, and Cam could work with and be in a relationship with their women, why couldn't he and Kenzie give it a shot? Who cared if they'd all bet on him falling for Kenzie--none of that seemed to matter anymore.

Although right now, she'd made it clear her entire focus was on work. "You know the flight's only an hour, right?"

"I do, but I've got a bunch of interviews this week and classes to plan for my trip to Denver on Thursday."

"Denver?"

"I'm flying out to film some new classes for YogaDownload. I'll be gone for a couple days. It's on the schedule I gave you our first day. You read it, right?" A crease formed between her brows.

Yeah, because he'd spent so much time studying it. Not. "I did, but I guess I forgot." And suddenly it was urgent they discuss their relationship.

He rose and crossed to the seat beside her. She turned to him, her mermaid eyes wide. "What are you doing?"

He placed one hand over her slim one. "Give me a couple minutes first, okay? We need to talk."

"Talk?"

His lips twitched. "Yeah. Since my parents stayed in Monterey, we have some privacy. It's going to be hectic once we get back to The Monroe, so I think we should define things between us now."

She swallowed and her gaze flickered down to where his hand still covered hers. "We can't just compartmentalize and deal with it later? You know we're both good at that."

He lifted his hand and caught her chin, angling her face gently toward him. "Yeah we are. And I don't want to compartmentalize anything with you. I think it's straightforward. We like each other. We like each other a lot."

Her lips curved up. "No question I like you. The timing is just tough."

"No timing is ever perfect, Kenzie. There are no guarantees, and I don't want to waste time. I think we're both capable of seeing each other and doing our jobs well, don't you?" Life was fucking short, and he'd never felt this way about anyone.

"I know that. But my plan was to get the spa up and

running, get settled here in Palm Springs, and *then* start dating. I have it on my vision board and everything."

He threw back his head and laughed. "You are priceless. Life doesn't work that way. Plans are great and all, but you never know what's around the corner. I never thought I'd be working with my big brother, running a hotel of all things."

She brushed one hand down his arm, then squeezed his forearm. "Yeah, you really did pivot, didn't you. I think your resiliency is amazing. You've bounced back and are doing something completely different. And you're doing it well."

"I don't know about that--I feel like I'm making it up as I go along. I have learned a lot working with everyone opening the other hotels. But it's different knowing at the end of the day, my name is on The Monroe."

"Aren't you worried I might distract you? You do have a lot riding on this opening. Don't you need to focus every-thing on it?"

He tucked a strand of her silky hair behind her ear. "You're already distracting. I think it would be way more fun to be distracted together instead of trying to pretend. Can you make a new vision board? Maybe one with both of us on it and then use your organizational superpowers to come up with an efficient schedule for us."

"Are you making fun of me?" She pouted.

He leaned in and pressed a kiss to her smooth cheek. "Never. I'm serious. I know I've teased you about it but I'm willing to take you any way I can get you. Why don't you work out a schedule for us--after work, overnights, whatev-er--that you're comfortable with. And if we've got time to be spontaneous in our free time, then that's all good too."

"You're serious about this aren't you?"

He caught both of her hands with his and gazed into her beautiful eyes. "Damn straight. You can even color code it. Change it week by week based on our schedules. I'll be able to focus on work a lot more if I know my reward is spending time with you. Kenzie, I want to get to know you better."

Her eyes gleamed and her face lit up like it was Christmas morning. "So, I can make you a color-coded folder and as long as it's about you and me spending sexy times together, you'll use it? Really?"

He hooked a pinky with hers. "Let's pinky swear. I, Austin Michaels, will review and comply with the sexy times schedule created by Kenzie Banks. But not just sexy times. I want to explore our new hometown, I want to take you out on dates, I want to hang out. Maybe even get you back on my bike. Cool?"

She linked her pinky with his. "You're a goofball. And maybe I'll consider the bike, but only on a deserted road where there's no traffic. I like you Austin and you're right. Not to be Debbie Downer, but do we have a plan for when this ends?"

His breath caught in his throat. "When it ends? Are you already giving us an expiration date?" *Play it cool, dude.*

She shifted back, and peered out the window, like a neon sign with answers would appear in the fluffy white clouds. "I'm not saying that. But like you said, we don't know what's around the corner. I'm just trying to be practical."

And she was right, even though he didn't like it. "I think we can handle it. I don't think it needs to be in writing. That would be weird. So, we're on?"

She turned and wound her arms around his neck. "Let's seal it with a kiss before I have to get to work."

He dropped his forehead against hers. "You may not have noticed on the ride here but there is a very nice bedroom in the back. We could make it official."

"You're incorrigible. I really do have to get a few things done right now. Time sensitive. So kiss me." She threaded her fingers through his hair and pressed her sweet mouth to his.

He slanted his mouth against hers and deepened the kiss, savoring her breath which tasted of mint and her unique flavor. Their tongues tangled in a leisurely dance, then he lifted his head. "So responsible. What about tonight?"

She sat back, her lips curving up into a small smile. "It would have to be late night because I'm fully booked this afternoon and evening choreographing new classes I'm filming."

He tugged on her silky ponytail. Imagined tugging it on it later when she was on her knees. "You drive a hard bargain. Deal."

"Or it would be really helpful if you were my guinea pig for a new yoga for athletes class. A private sunset yoga session work for you?"

"Will you be wearing one of those sexy little crop tops and leggings?" He waggled his eyebrows.

She laughed and rolled her eyes. "Why yes, I will. But just yoga, no fooling around. I should have already completed these class plans."

He pressed a hand to his heart and sighed. "I'll do it. Will I get brownie points or a special checkmark on our schedule? Like a gold star?"

"Maybe if you're very good." Her smile was broad. "Let me work on it now though, okay?"

He pressed a quick kiss to her soft pink lips and fetched his own laptop. God knows he had enough work to keep him occupied. And he couldn't let anything else slip through the cracks.

He could be patient. Now she'd agreed to see where their relationship would go. Even though he could likely charm her into making out for the rest of the flight, he wanted her to be happy. And he'd already figured out, she needed structure. He could adapt. She was worth it.

~

KENZIE SET up Austin's yoga mat facing hers on the wide poolside patio and checked her watch. He was due in ten minutes, enough time to gather her composure. She sat cross-legged on her mat, rested her hands on her thighs, and allowed her eyes to drift shut.

Her emotions tangled in her chest. Every moment they spent together deepened her attraction to him. Because very few people saw the real her and Austin's piercing midnight gaze penetrated beneath her carefully cultivated exterior.

Austin's openness and honesty had surprised her this morning. Unafraid to declare he liked her, not just for the sex, and wanted to pursue things. Maybe the wedding had illuminated for him how other couples were working together and in love.

In love. Holy cow. Had she truly come up with the "L" word again?

She shivered and rubbed the goosebumps erupting on her arms. In the 80 degree afternoon. One thing was for sure--whatever was happening between them wasn't casual. Was she brave enough to take it day by day, like he'd suggested? To set aside her fears and embrace the present moment--like she preached to her yoga students on the regular.

"Yoga model, reporting for duty." Austin's rasped in his deep voice.

Her eyes flew open and there he stood, looking a little sheepish, and adorably boyish. His black hair flopped across his strong brow and her fingers itched to smooth it away from the chiseled perfection of his features. He wore loose board shorts, thank god, and a faded Stone Temple Pilots t-shirt.

Her mouth grew parched, but she was a professional, right? No drooling over hot students allowed. "Right on time, too. Have a seat."

He easily dropped to his mat and mirrored her position. "Yes teacher."

"Ooh, I like when my students address me as teacher. One brownie point for you." She'd borrow a page from his casual humor playbook.

"I'm ready when you are."

She stepped into her teacher role. "Okay, this is a thirty minute Yoga for Athletes class. I designed it to complement any sports."

"Some stretching can do all that?"

"Yoga isn't just stretching. A well-rounded yoga practice includes dynamic flexibility training, core stabilization, strengthening, and balance work. Great to counterbalance all kinds of workouts."

"So like with golfers and tennis players overdeveloping one side of their bodies?"

"Exactly. Another gold star for you." She grinned at him. "Yeah, it's also great to develop mental focus and concentration––a lot of the pro athletes use it. Ready?"

"Be gentle with me. I've only tried yoga a few times and it didn't go well."

"You'll be fine. Just do what I tell you."

He licked his lips. "Hmmm…you know I love your bossy side."

She shook a finger at him. "Be good. I really need to run through this to make sure it flows. So we'll start in child's pose to stretch out your back and settle into your breath. Spread your knees wide to the edges of your mat, with your big toes touching and walk your hands out in front."

He complied and she absolutely did *not* ogle the way the fabric of his t-shirt strained across the sinewy muscles of his back. Or those forearms laid out on the mat, begging to be stroked. With effort, she lifted her gaze toward the deep violet outline of the mountain range and the hovering sun ready to slip behind it.

Go time. Over the next thirty minutes, she guided him through Sun Salutations, linked standing poses from Warrior 1 to Triangle Pose and Extended Side Angle. Then she challenged his balance with a fun Eagle Pose to Standing Splits ending in Wide Straddle Forward Fold. Of course he flowed through, graceful and powerful like a panther.

Once he was reclining in Savasana, or corpse pose, she indulged herself and admired him. Reclined and relaxed, his sooty eyelashes lay like fans on his high cheekbones, his square jaw was relaxed, his beautiful mouth soft and kissable. His long lean frame was too tempting––class was over after all––so she knelt next to him and pressed her lips to his.

Without warning, he reached up and yanked her down on top of him, banding his powerful arms around her. She sprawled inelegantly across his hard, hot body, a tremor of awareness sparking down her spine. "Hey!"

He slid one hand up to the back of her head and met her mouth in a deep, passionate kiss. Her heart knocked against her ribs, her nipples tightened, and her hips rocked against the steel ridge of his erection. His rough hands stroked her back and caught her bottom, holding her closer.

"You taste so good," she murmured against his lips. Smelled delicious. Felt dangerous. Temptation personified.

He slid one hand into the waistband of her yoga pants, and flames shot straight down to her core when his calloused fingers stroked her skin. Their faces were inches apart, their breath mingling in sharp harsh pants. Austin's eyes were hooded, his pupils so dilated the irises were bottomless black pools.

"Yeah? I want to taste all of you. Come back to my room with me."

She moistened her lips. No way could she resist. She'd gotten her work done, right? Time for her reward. "Yes."

He shifted, rolled them to the side, and pressed up to standing. "See, look how limber I am now, teacher."

"Mmm-hmm."

He scooped her up, one arm cradling her shoulders, the other hooked under her knees. She wrapped one arm around his neck, thrusting her fingers into his soft, thick mane. Who knew a guy's hair could be so sexy?

Continuing to keep their lips locked, Austin strode to his suite and carried her straight to the bed. He gently laid her back on the mountain of pillows and raked his gaze over her. "You're so beautiful."

Her throat tightened at the tenderness in his eyes, the sincerity in his voice.

He shifted back and tugged off his t-shirt with one hand, revealing the gleaming skin covering his sculpted chest and abs.

"You're the beautiful one. Don't just stand there, come here." She extended one hand.

Heat flared in his eyes, and he caught her hand, intertwining their fingers together. He lifted their joined hands to his mouth and kissed each knuckle, without breaking their gaze. Her heart thundered against her ribcage.

He knelt between her legs, slid one hand behind her head and lowered his mouth to hers. His tongue swept lazily with hers, his movements languid, unhurried. Her eyelids floated shut as he trailed open-mouthed kisses along her jaw and down her neck. Heat curled down her spine and she reached for him, eager to feel his full weight on her.

He shifted back and she moaned in protest. "You've got way too many clothes on."

She propped up onto her elbows and together they got her sports bra off and tossed it aside. He groaned, lowered his dark head and captured one nipple in his mouth, licking and setting her aflame.

"Please…" She dug her fingers into his hair, holding his head in place.

"I've got you." His calloused hands glided up and cupped her breasts, pushing them together. Kissing, teasing, licking her until her back bowed up.

Her head dropped back into the pillows and sparks danced along her skin. She needed more. She wrapped her legs around his hips and pulled him until he was flush against her center.

He groaned and slid one hand down to curve around her hip, rocking into her. "Let's get rid of these."

They rolled to the side, and she wiggled out of her yoga pants before reaching for the strings of his board shorts. In a flash, they were gone, and he was on her again.

He spread her legs apart with firm hands, then stroked one finger along her center. He growled. "You're so ready for me."

"I want you inside me."

He slid two fingers inside her, and pleasure surged through her. "I'm going to take good care of you, baby." He increased his pace, pressed his palm against her and in one, two, three strokes, she came apart, his name on her lips.

He lifted his mouth to hers again, his kiss tender, almost sweet. She stroked her fingernails down the smooth lines of his back and grabbed his perfect butt in her hands. He tensed, his rock hard erection digging against her hip.

"Please Austin, I want you."

He hissed out a harsh breath, rolled off her, and grabbed a

condom from the nightstand. He knelt between her legs, caught both her hands, and pressed them down onto the bed. He lined himself up and slowly, inch by inch, filled her to bursting.

Their harsh pants filled the air and for a moment, he remained motionless. Time stood still. He slanted his mouth against hers and began to move. They found a slow, dreamy rhythm and he never stopped kissing her. Their skin grew slick, and each stroke ratcheted the sensations rocketing through her body higher.

When he changed the angle, hitting that magic spot inside of her, the orgasm exploded through her in long, undulating waves. He dropped his head and bit lightly on the spot where her neck and shoulder met.

"Kenzie." He breathed her name and followed her over the edge.

After a few moments, he cradled her in his arms and turned them onto their sides, facing each other. He smoothed her damp hair away from her face, his indigo eyes searching before dropping his forehead against hers.

She breathed in his masculine scent, savoring the feel of him. Tonight they'd moved beyond the wild passion that had connected them so far.

Tonight felt like they'd crossed an intimate line––one from which she wasn't sure they could return. She squashed the flicker of anxiety that moved through her. Austin wasn't a bad boy, like her ex-boyfriends. They had taken this step together with eyes wide open. Nothing to worry about it if they took it day by day.

CHAPTER 19

Austin strode to the lobby where he was meeting Kenzie for their first real date. His brother and Jon were arriving the day after tomorrow, so he'd made reservations for an intimate, romantic dinner at Mastro's. He was feeling pretty damn smug—who said he couldn't run a hotel and have a fulfilling relationship with the most fascinating woman he'd ever met?

June was passing in a blur of busier than hell days and hotter than hell nights with Kenzie. And so far, they'd both been able to focus on work and each other. Mostly.

Well, except for a minor screw-up with one of the shower tile vendors. Maybe he'd gotten distracted after a few scorching phone calls with Kenzie when she was in Denver. He'd forgotten to sign the purchase order by the deadline, but it had all worked out.

And maybe he'd begged Lucas to finish a few extra reports he hadn't completed on time. Nothing serious. He had it all handled, and Ryan was none the wiser. Nothing important had slid through the cracks.

"Hello handsome." Kenzie sauntered toward him on long

shapely legs, showcased by sky-high stilettos and a short white dress.

Yeah, she looked amazing in the morning with a bare face and tangled hair, rocked her yoga clothes like a queen, but tonight she was a Greek goddess with her tumble of burnished red-gold hair, dramatic eye-makeup, and creamy skin.

"HEY GORGEOUS." Every muscle in his body sprang to attention. For a split second he considered throwing her tight little body over his shoulder and ditching the reservations.

She wound her arms around his neck and lifted her face for a kiss. "Thanks for setting up this evening. I love getting dressed up every once in a while. Especially with such a handsome date."

He lowered his head and captured her mouth. Her lip gloss tasted like strawberries and mixed with her own special flavor… *holy hell, he was in trouble.* But he'd promised to take her out and she was excited about it so, fancy dinner date it would be.

"You'll love Mastro's. It's over in Palm Desert, a solid twenty minute drive. And don't worry, we're taking the Mustang, not the bike." They headed toward the parking lot.

She snorted. "Ha ha. As if I'd ride a motorcycle in a dress. If and when I ever ride that machine again, it won't be in a fancy outfit."

He caught her hand and intertwined his fingers with hers. "I promise we'll take her for a fun ride on some back roads, and you'll fall for her too."

Traffic was light on the palm tree lined streets, and he pulled up at the valet station right on time. Walking in, he placed his hand on Kenzie's bare lower back, whispering a silent thank you for the way the fabric draped just above her perfect butt. The restaurant's entrance was like entering a wine cave, with floor to ceiling mahogany wood wine cabinets. An almost infinitesimal number of bottles were backlit and displayed behind gleaming glass fronts. They even had moving ladders to access the top racks, like in those old-fashioned libraries.

A black-suited whippet of a maître'd escorted them to a secluded corner table with white-tablecloths and polished china settings. Warm amber walls and wood-beamed ceilings kept the classic steakhouse's ambiance welcoming. The golden lighting of the restaurant only served to emphasize her beauty and underscore the goddess vibe she channeled tonight.

The waiter materialized next to the table, with suggestions for cocktails and details on the nightly specials. Kenzie chose her customary seltzer water with lemon, and he selected the same.

She laid one hand over his. "You know I don't mind if you have a drink, there's no need to have water like me."

"I don't need to have alcohol with every meal. Plus, I want to see why you love your seltzer with lemon so much."

Her eyes crinkled at the corners, and she squeezed his hand. "Okay, just so you know, please never apologize for drinking, okay?"

He nodded and when the waiter returned, they ordered their meals.

"So, since this is officially our first date, we should ask some first date questions, right?" Kenzie said.

He froze, his glass halfway to his lips. "First date questions? Like favorite foods and hobbies and stuff?"

"Among other things. I mean, we've shared some really deep personal things from our pasts but less of the day to day." She glanced around the restaurant and leaned in closer.

"Not to mention, most people haven't had incredible sex up against the wall before their first dates."

He coughed and grabbed his glass and chugged some ice water.

She giggled and patted him on the back. "Did I surprise you?"

A smile tugged at his lips, and he slid one hand under the table and stroked her toned thigh. "I thought you were going to ask me for my favorite color. And on a first date, you might slap me if I did this, right?" he whispered.

Her breath hitched and she caught her lower lip in her straight white teeth. "Mmm-hmm. Maybe. Maybe not."

He indulged himself with one more caress of her warm silky skin before sitting back. Damn it, he wanted to learn more about her. "Okay, let's play. My favorite color is turquoise, my birthday is December 19th, my favorite food is Mexican. I would do anything for my family. I dislike reptiles but I love cats and dogs. Your turn."

"Hmmm, I didn't know any of those things except for how close you are to your family. My favorite color is purple, specifically violet, my birthday is July 30th, which makes us both fire signs––Sagittarius and Leo––which explains a lot." Color rose in her cheeks. "Italian food for me. I love all animals, except for spiders."

One omission stood out. He reached out and clasped her slender hand in his. "This might be a lot for a first date conversation, but I think it can be an exception. You told me about your mom but didn't really speak about your dad. Is he in the picture?"

Her full lips flattened. "I hate to think about either of them, but I'll tell you. Both of my parents are alcoholics, which is why I rarely if ever drink. My dad is basically a functioning one, going off to his corporate job every day and drinking in front of the television at night until he passes out. Let's just say, he didn't pay much attention to me except if I got in his line of vision when he was in a mood."

"Did he hurt you?" His gut clenched.

"He didn't hit me if that's what you're asking. He just wasn't a father to me, besides providing the appropriate ingredients to my mother." She dropped her gaze to her plate, pushing the salad around with the tines of her fork.

"But you grew up with two addicts for parents, so you never really got the chance to be a kid because you had to either take care of or stay out of the way of them, right?" Her schedules and lists and charts made more sense now––they gave her a sense of self-control.

She gazed up at him, her eyes wide. "How did you get to be so wise? Because yeah, that about sums it up. But so many people have it worse than I did."

"Don't do that. We're talking about you. Being around addicts is tough, especially as a child. I'm sorry."

"Thank you. It's really nice to see how close your family is. You're lucky. You and Chris seem close, even if he isn't your real dad."

"Chris is great, but he wasn't around until a few years after my dad died. Ryan felt like he needed to step in and take care of me and Grant."

She turned her hand over and intertwined her fingers with his. "I'm so sorry. And that explains Ryan's CEO personality."

"Yeah, he had to grow up fast––kind of like you. But then Chris hired my mom to manage the house at Pacific Vista Ranch. We went from this normal middle-class neighborhood to a two-hundred and twenty acre ranch in Rancho Santa Fe."

"Isn't Rancho Santa Fe that fancy exclusive community north of San Diego?"

"Yeah. You'll have to come out to the ranch sometime. It's

heaven on earth. Anyway, after a few years, Chris and my mom fell in love and got married, so we became kind of like the Brady Bunch."

Her face lit up. "I love that Angela and Chris got a second chance at love. Chris seems like he's been an incredible father figure for all of you."

"Yeah, we're lucky. And you sure turned out well for not having that kind of support." But damn the conversation had gotten more serious than he'd anticipated. Diving deep seemed to be their natural way of relating.

"Aww, thanks. Teaching yoga has helped me because I used to throw myself into unhealthy relationships, kind of replicating patterns, you know? So now I nurture my students instead of trying to take care of people who are emotional vampires."

Little puzzle pieces about her were falling into place. "Now who is the wise one? You're an amazing teacher and an even more amazing woman."

"Why thank you. Okay, switching gears. Favorite movie. Favorite book. Favorite place you've ever been. Oh, and favorite candy. Mine is anything chocolate with mint."

"Chocolate mint for me too--anything from those Girl Scout cookies to ice cream, to peppermint patties. Favorite movie is a tie between *Almost Famous* and *Inglorious Bastards*. I've got a lot of favorite books--anything from Hemingway to Stephen King to Anne LaMott."

"Oh, I love both those movies. My favorite is probably *Pride and Prejudice*, the Keira Knightly version and for comedy, nothing beats *Horrible Bosses*." She waved one hand. "My favorite place I've traveled is the Cinque Terre in Italy. It's heaven. Tell me yours and we can stop the lists."

"I like hearing about everything you love. My favorite city is Paris. Something about it just felt like home. But we forgot one thing. I know you aren't huge into alt-rock, so what's your favorite music?"

Her brows drew together as she considered her response. "It's not that I don't like it, I just haven't listened to tons of it beyond the 90s stuff, like with Soundgarden and Pearl Jam. I guess I'm more old school. I like some more classic bands, like from the 60s and 70s. Fleetwood Mac, The Doors, Queen. But I also like dance music."

"I like the classics too. I'll just have to help expand your horizons." He winked.

Before she could respond, the waiter returned with her halibut and his filet mignon. Everything looked and smelled delicious. Kind of like Kenzie. And there his brain went again. The more time he spent with her, the more attracted he became. He admired how resilient she was and how much she'd accomplished without having anyone backing her up.

Their banter grew more flirtatious as they made it through a dark chocolate mousse and asked for the check.

He settled the bill and asked, "Ready to go?" He couldn't wait to get back to The Monroe with her.

"I'm ready for you. How quickly can you get us home?" Her blue-green eyes were heavy-lidded, her lips parted.

Home. Something about her reference to the hotel where they were living together flooded his chest with unfamiliar sensations of tenderness and protectiveness. He shot up from the table, grabbed her hand, and sprinted for the exit.

"If I had my bike, we'd already be in my bed. But I'll risk a speeding ticket."

She slid one arm around his waist and matched his pace. "I'm down with that because the faster you drive, the sooner I can get you naked."

He was rock hard again, and his breath hissed through his teeth. Luck was with them, and the valet had his Mustang at the curb. Now if he could keep it together to drive now that every drop of blood had dropped south of his waist.

They dove into the car, buckled up, and he peeled off down the street with a squeal of tires. She curled her long fingers around his thigh and urged him to hurry. He navigated to the back streets and broke every single speed limit to reach The Monroe.

CHAPTER 20

$\mathcal{K}$enzie checked off the final item on her hiring spreadsheet, leapt out of her seat, and danced around her suite. It was the third week of June, and she had every single employee hired for the spa, save the cleaning crew. Nothing like completing one of her primary goals a week early. And she'd received a check from her insurance company--she'd be able to replace her VW and stop borrowing Austin's Mustang.

Ryan and Jon had been at The Monroe for a week and were heading back to San Diego tomorrow. Neither had seemed surprised or concerned she and Austin were together. Not like they could have hidden their feelings, even if they tried. So much for being master compartmentalizers.

Instead of distracting her from her work, spending all her free time with Austin was actually resulting in her being more productive. Go figure--when she had plans with someone she loved being with, she was able to focus more and work less. A first for her.

Every moment they spent together, she tumbled deeper under his spell. Sure, he was charismatic and charming and entertaining. But each day, he revealed more of the sensitive artistic soul residing beneath his easygoing exterior. He made her feel like she was the most special person in the world--he saw beneath her surface too--something they had in common.

Her earlier fears of getting involved with him seemed laughable now. She'd never been happier on every level. Her dream career was rolling along, she was falling for an incredible man, and not that she was planning too far out, but it felt like they were building The Monroe together. Building a new life together.

She checked her watch. Five minutes until a meeting with Ryan, Jon, and Austin to review timelines and plans to ensure a smooth opening Labor Day weekend. Because Austin's room boasted a bigger living room/office area, complete with a small conference table, they were gathering there. Humming to herself, she smoothed back her high ponytail, grabbed her portfolio, and strolled out of her room.

Before she reached Austin's room, angry voices assaulted her ears. What the heck? She ran to the suite's open door and her jaw dropped.

Ryan and Austin faced off in the middle of the room, faces red, fists clenched. Jon stood several feet away, looking nervously between the two brothers.

"Were you planning on telling me, hell, telling anybody, before you bailed or were you just going to take off like you did in high school?" Ryan's voice was low and deadly calm.

Austin threw up his hands. "I told you the story's bullshit. But of course you assumed it was true."

"Well, your guitar player made it pretty damn clear when he said the band was thrilled you were coming back and were heading into the studio next month to record a new album."

Austin narrowed his dark eyes. "Liam's full of it. I told him I wasn't coming back."

"Told him? So, you have been discussing it with him?"

Austin dragged a hand through his shaggy hair. "If you'd listen to me for a damn minute, I'd tell you."

Ryan's jaw was tight. "Excuse me if I don't have the most faith in you. It's not like I didn't have to twist your arm to be part of Hotel Kings to begin with."

A flicker of something passed over Austin's face before he quickly masked it. "Thanks so much. I've been working my ass off for you since last year and doing a damn good job here."

Ryan glared at his younger brother. "Do you want a medal? We're all working our asses off. But everyone else is all in and it sure seems like you've got one foot out the door already."

Jon stepped up between them. "You guys need to stop. This isn't helping." He pointed at Ryan. "Ryan, control your temper and let Austin explain."

He turned to Austin and wagged a finger. "The story looks really bad and it's all over the internet. So don't be so defensive and explain." Jon crossed his arms and looked between the brothers expectantly.

Nobody had noticed her in the doorway. What in the world had happened? Her shoulders tensed and her she pressed her hands to her churning belly.

Austin's nostrils flared. "I would think you'd remember not everything you read online or hear in the news is true. Liam approached me and asked me to come back. I told him no. He's called a few more times but I haven't spoken to him since last month. Nothing's changed on my end."

"Why would he give this interview and announcement if there wasn't any truth to it? You need to tell me if there's anything behind it."

"You know what, Ryan? You can go fuck yourself. I'm not a liar and you know it. I was all in for this gig but now I see just how much faith you have in me, maybe I should bail. At least nobody in the music world questions my talent and my loyalty, like you do. I need some air."

With that pronouncement, Austin stalked out of the room. His eyes widened a fraction when he saw her, "I need to clear my head."

And he disappeared down the hallway without a backward glance. Leaving without any explanation or apology.

"Kenzie, I didn't see you there," Ryan said, his jaw tight. "Sorry about the scene."

Jon approached her. "How much did you hear?"

She ran her tongue around her teeth. "Enough. What's going on? What's this news story?" It wasn't awkward demanding answers from her CEO, who was her lover boss's brother. Nope, not one little bit.

Ryan sighed and rubbed his square jaw, so like his brother's. "Let's sit down."

Nerves skittered down her spine. She wouldn't believe the worst of Austin, at least until she spoke with him and got the full story. But what if Austin's fight with Ryan caused him to quit? Everything between them had been going so smoothly. Maybe too smoothly.

She joined Ryan and Jon at the small round table. She set down her notebook and folded her hands in her lap. Waited.

"I'm sorry you had to see that lack of professionalism. One of the downsides of working with family. I guess you have questions?"

Well, at least he wasn't going to interrogate her. Now she was seeing Ryan's fierce side. He was kind of scary. "Could you explain what all that was about?"

"Yeah. The biggest news story of the day is that Black Velvet Machine is back together, Austin is returning, and they're headed to the studio and on tour early next year. Let's just say I didn't take it well."

Jon interjected, "Ryan doesn't like surprises."

Obviously. She merely nodded and gestured for him to continue. Her stomach twisted into knots. No way could she reconcile the sweet man she'd been falling in love with over the last month with a guy who was lying to everyone.

Ryan's stoic expression turned sheepish. "Maybe I over-reacted. But Austin wasn't much help explaining why this story is everywhere."

Jon rolled his eyes and pressed one hand to his chest. "Maybe? You lit into him before he had a chance to say a word. Just let him cool off and you two will work it out."

Ryan pinched the bridge of his nose. "Kenzie, I'm not trying to put you in the middle but did Austin mention anything about the band to you? Did the guys come out here?"

She stiffened. "That does actually put me in an awkward position, but I've got nothing to hide and neither does he. As far as I know, none of the band members have visited nor did he mention seeing them."

Or talking to them, which he did admit to Ryan. Why hadn't he mentioned it? Had he been considering returning?

A sliver of doubt sliced through her. It wasn't like he had to disclose every conversation he had but his former band pressuring him to return did seem like a major omission. They'd been spending every night together and he hadn't breathed a word about it.

Growing up with her parents who basically lied to the world about who they really were, she generally could spot dishonesty quickly. Had her attraction to Austin colored her perception?

Ryan gave a curt nod, then opened his laptop. "Okay, that's good. Well, Austin won't be back for a while but we'll sort it out. Jon and I need to get back to La Jolla tonight so let's go ahead and review the details for Sanctuary Spa. Are you ready?"

Apparently all the Michaels brothers could compartmentalize. And so could she. Ensuring Ryan had the utmost confidence in her ability to run the spa had to be her primary focus. She tucked away her fears about Austin in that inner space where she crammed all the matters she didn't care to deal with immediately.

She took a cleansing breath. "Absolutely. I emailed you both the spreadsheets. Go ahead and open the budget tab, it's the first one."

And notwithstanding the pit in her belly, they focused on business.

CHAPTER 21

$\mathcal{A}$ustin stalked into his ensuite bathroom, with its extra-large silver tiles, mirrored wall, and a walk-in shower big enough for a party of six, looking for his keys. Not that he was in the mood to appreciate the room's design.

Screw his big brother--he could read and analyze all the damn reports on his own. The reports he'd worked hours on with Lucas, eager to show his brother how well everything was shaping up for The Monroe. *Screw him.*

Right now, he needed his motorcycle. After the ugly scene with Ryan and the overwhelming desire to murder Liam, he needed the powerful engine beneath him, some speed, and the wind in his face.

Time to cruise up into the mountains and get away from this godforsaken desert. He changed into a pair of light-weight pants and grabbed his leather jacket. Despite the hundred degree heat, he still needed the protection, especially once he'd reached the San Jacinto Mountains. Cruising ninety miles an hour on his Harley would cool him off.

He reached his bike without seeing a soul. Not that he was in the mood to talk. Not until he'd had a chance to think.

Craig and the construction crew were working on the spa interior this week, and it wasn't like his brother had followed him to apologize. And he hadn't exactly invited Kenzie to follow him.

A flash of regret passed through him. She didn't deserve the drama. Knowing Ryan and his ability to be a freakin' robot, they were reviewing numbers and charts right now. Would she assume the story was true? Or would she give him a chance to explain, unlike his brother? Would she trust him?

He swung a leg over his bike and started the engine. The sweet purr of the motor soothed the tension cloaking his shoulders. Without glancing back at the hotel he'd devoted the lion's share of his time to over the last months, he charged toward freedom.

He wove through the light early afternoon traffic until he reached the turn straight up into the rocky, winding roads. With every mile, his ability to focus sharpened. Ryan's immediate doubt and conclusions stung. Nah, not just a slight sting, but a stabbing pain. Like his big brother had anticipated him screwing up.

Maybe he was the kind of person who ran in times of trouble instead of sticking. He'd left Black Velvet Machine when tragedy struck. Had he abandoned the other guys by not staying with the band like Liam claimed? Liam acted like it was a sign of weakness to walk away instead of fighting to stay together. Maybe he had failed them. Maybe he'd failed Tommy.

His fingers dug into the handlebars. Damn it, no, he hadn't quit the band out of weakness or lack of work ethic, he'd quit because his heart had broken when Tommy died. They had started the band together and with him gone? His heart was no longer in it. And if he wasn't passionately committed to whatever he was doing, he couldn't do it at all.

He had to be all in.

And he'd committed to the Hotel Kings. Committed to his big brother--poured his heart into the new venture from Day One, despite his doubts. Over the last year, he had proven his worth as the hotel chain's Food and Beverage Manager. He'd done his best over the last months as the GM of The Monroe.

Did the rest of the team see him as a flight risk, the way Ryan seemed to? Maybe they had all been expecting him to fail but humored him because of Ryan. Hell, he was the only one on the team who hadn't come from a corporate background.

Even though he'd screwed up a few times, they were only minor issues. He'd believed he was doing a good job and was enjoying it. Especially working with Kenzie.

The doubt in his big brother's eyes triggered memories of when he was the rebellious teenager, always getting in trouble. Always having his mom or Chris bail him out of his latest scrape. Was that how Ryan still saw him deep down?

His forced himself to soften his death grip on the handles. Maybe it was time to reconsider all of it. Maybe he *was* a square peg in a round hole. Sure, he could do the GM job but was he the best person for it?

Maybe Liam's chess move trying to manipulate him to return to the rock and roll world was a sign. Should he be singing and following his lifelong passion? It was what he did best. Was he really running away and choosing a career that he *could* do but wasn't his true calling because he'd failed Tommy?

But over these last weeks with Kenzie, the notes had returned to him. His heart was bursting with music. His notebook was crammed with words. Not just words.

Lyrics. Lyrics about her and the way she made him feel. Lyrics from his heart. Songs he could sing with his acoustic guitar. Could perform at The Monroe or small venues on his own. And having the well open again hadn't enticed him to rejoin the band again or live that hectic lifestyle.

Thoughts and emotions flooded through him as he surrendered to the rhythm of the road. Riding was like meditation for him––often where he'd have bursts of clarity or sparks of inspiration when the music wasn't flowing. He leaned into the turns, cruised the curves of the almost deserted mountain streets and allowed a sense of calm to wash over him.

The decision for his future was crystal clear. He'd enjoy a long ride and make sure he didn't return to the hotel until Ryan had headed back to San Diego. He'd call his brother. A phone call would be fine––no need to have another confrontation.

He crested the sharp curve to the small mom and pop restaurant that had the best soft-serve ice cream in the world. He'd grab a zebra cone, then head back and explain his decision to Kenzie. He didn't want any secrets between them.

When he turned into the parking lot, a horn squealed, and he jerked the bike to the right to avoid the red pick-up truck barreling straight toward him. He crashed into a row of shrubbery and cacti and cut the engine with a curse. At least the barrier had prevented him from crashing into the asphalt––he'd done that before and had the road rash scar to prove it.

"Oh my goodness, are you okay?" A middle-aged woman rushed toward him.

He righted his bike and considered for a moment. Nothing was broken anyway. "Yeah, I'm fine. But where's the driver?"

The parking lot was empty except for a single silver sedan.

Her eyes narrowed and she put her hands on her hips.

"That hooligan didn't bother to stop. Just peeled out of here after cutting through our parking lot to avoid the intersection at the stop sign. But you're bleeding so you come inside with me."

He blew out an unsteady breath. "I'm fine, just a few scratches. What I really want is one of your soft-serve cones."

"Of course. I've got a first aid kit, so you'll come in and clean up those scratches and I'll get you that ice cream. Follow me." She turned and headed toward the low-slung wooden building.

He removed his helmet, scrubbed through his sweaty hair, and fell into step beside her. Yeah, once he'd washed up, it was time to cruise home and make it clear to everyone in his life what he wanted.

AUSTIN PARKED his bike at The Monroe and strode toward the entrance of his hotel. Before he crossed the lobby's threshold, Ryan appeared, his expression impassive. *Shit.* He'd counted on his brother being gone by now.

"We need to talk. Just you and me. The bar or your room?" Ryan's tone brooked no argument.

Austin squared his shoulders. "Where are Jon and Kenzie?"

"Jon's in the pool and Kenzie's working. The bar or your room?"

His gut churned. "Let's go to the bar."

They marched to the bar without speaking. No need to make another scene because he had a feeling this might not be a calm discussion. Although his brother rarely raised his voice, Ryan's quiet words could be more devastating than the yelling matches Austin had experienced with the band.

They entered the lounge but right now, he didn't want an

icy beer, he just wanted to get this conversation behind him, for better or for worse. He headed straight to a booth, slid onto the smooth leather seat, and Ryan sat across from him.

He stared at his usually unflappable brother and waited.

Ryan cleared his throat and met his gaze. "You okay?"

"What do you want to talk about, Ryan?" If his brother was going to rail him, he wanted to get it over with.

"I want to apologize."

Austin froze. "What?"

"Apologize. I owe you an apology. I over-reacted earlier and was an asshole."

"What's the deal with that? You didn't even give me a chance to get a word in edgewise." He tamped down the flare of irritation.

Ryan rubbed the scruff on his jaw. "Look, I'm not perfect, okay?"

"Seriously? But you always have been the perfect one. You never fuck up. Not even when we were kids." At least after their dad died.

Ryan barked out a harsh laugh. "Yeah, right. I fuck up all the time, I'm just better at covering it up."

"You assumed the story was valid because you think I'm a fuck-up. I've always been the one who lets people down and you're the one who handles everything, no matter what."

"Austin, that's not true. Yeah, you were a wild kid and ran away to be in a rock and roll band. But you're so freakin' talented you became a star. I've always been proud of you, but..."

"But?"

Ryan blew out a breath. "Don't take this the wrong way but I worry about you. You've always been the most sensitive one in the family and I know you feel things hard. I know you felt guilty about not being able to save Tommy, but nobody could have saved him, okay?"

A stab of pain pierced his heart. "Maybe I could have. Maybe if I hadn't--"

"No. No you couldn't, and you know it deep down. And I don't know, maybe Liam had manipulated you into believing Tommy would have wanted you to keep playing and you didn't know how to tell me. I don't know."

For a few moments, neither of them spoke. Had Ryan lashed out because he was worried?

"So you didn't assume I was bailing because I'm irresponsible?" Because he had been an irresponsible teenager, always looking for trouble.

"No. Look, you know me better than almost anyone. I would never have asked you to join the Hotel Kings if I didn't think you would be great at it. Okay?"

"You think I'm great at it?" His breath hitched.

Ryan nodded. "You're a natural--well, except for the numbers, but the best managers surround themselves with people who are experts. And we'll all make mistakes. I mean, hell, remember what a mess I made with the ballroom situation with Charlie?"

Austin chuckled. "Yeah, she's amazing and she was right. That woman is the best thing to ever happen to you, professionally and personally." He'd never seen his serious brother happier.

"Yes she is. But I want to make sure we've cleared the air. Are you happy here? Do you think about going back?"

"Yeah, of course I've thought about returning. Music has been my life since I was 17. I didn't think I'd end up here, but this is where I want to be. It feels right, and I've still got music."

"Yeah?"

"I've been writing again. And I don't need to go on tour or play with a band to make music. I can play some acoustic sets here, hell, maybe even sell some of the songs."

Ryan's lips curved up. "That's great. You made our wedding really special and the acoustic music under the stars series is going to make this place stand out. So, we good?"

"We're good. Want a beer?" A flush rose in his cheeks from the praise. The approval.

"I do. Jon's driving us home, but I've got time for a drink with my baby brother."

Austin rose, crossed to the bar, grabbed two local lagers, and cracked them open. He set down the icy bottles on the table and sat.

They tapped bottles and drank.

Ryan quirked a brow. "Now that's settled, I have one more question."

"What's that?"

"I'm assuming you're writing again because of Kenzie. So can I go tell everyone we won the bet and you two are an official couple?"

Austin closed his eyes and counted to five. "Seriously? I get Jack and Jon and even Cam getting in on the bet, but you?"

Ryan leaned in close. "Come on, if you tell me first, I'll get the cash. I'll split it with you."

"Between you and me? I'm crazy about her but I need to talk to her next, especially after the scene this afternoon. That's something she'll have to answer."

"Go get on that, little brother. She's a keeper."

Austin's chest tightened. But would she want to keep him after today?

CHAPTER 22

*K*enzie paced around the perimeter of her spacious suite for the twelfth time. It was past 5 p.m. and she hadn't heard from Austin yet. No response to any of her texts. Maybe he was taking a local ride, but he could be to San Francisco by now or Mexico.

Once she'd finished the meeting with Ryan and Jon, she'd hurried back to her room and read the interview and articles splashed all over the web. The return of Black Velvet Machine was a huge deal in the entertainment industry and sure enough, the band claimed Austin was back. It wasn't an interview implying Austin *might* return. No, Liam and the other guys stated Austin was tying up some loose ends and meeting them in the studio in mid-July.

No wonder Ryan had lost it.

Why would the band lie? Usually when people claimed stories were false, there was a hint of truth. Austin had admitted he'd talked to Liam a few times. Was he weighing his options and Liam assumed he'd choose the band? Had she been reckless by trusting him too soon?

She threw herself down on the mid-century suede

loveseat in her suite, curled up and hugged her knees into her chest. She'd been so positive she and Austin were falling in love. She was in love with him--no doubts there. No matter that she'd tried to break her former relationship patterns, had she messed up and chosen poorly again?

All day her stomach had been in knots, she hadn't been able to eat, and her mother's nasty voice played in her head. Reminding her that she wasn't good enough, that she was like her good for nothing father and she'd end up just like her, with a loser husband and nothing to show for her hard work.

No. Just no. She sat up and redid her ponytail. Damn it, she would never be like her mother. She was a success, despite her mother. And she wasn't careless like her father.

Wasn't that one of the driving forces of her life? That she'd be successful and happy and have a wonderful family despite her parents. Maybe even a little bit to spite them.

Sanctuary Spa was her dream and regardless of what happened with Austin--stay or go--she would remain here and create the life of her dreams. She'd already made friends with everyone, bonding at the bachelorette party and the wedding. She and Lucy talked on the phone often, as did she and Campbell. No man would ruin her life, even if he broke her heart. She was resilient and strong, and she would navigate to a happy ending, with or without him.

A sob escaped her. But wouldn't it be lovely if it was with him? She trusted him and wished he would get his butt back here and explain. She'd listen with an open mind. If he ended up leaving, well, just one more lesson to add to the list.

Where was he? He couldn't have simply bailed and gone to L.A., could he?

Unable to stand the confinement of the four walls, she threw on her swimsuit and grabbed a towel. She'd swim some laps and try to quiet her mind. Time was inching along so she may as well fill it with something productive. Sitting in her room crying wasn't going to bring him back.

She marched outside, enjoying the warm air caressing her skin. She tossed the towel and her phone on one of the new lounge chairs and dove into the pool. She powered through the cool water, her strokes and kicks fueled by frustration and hurt. Lap after lap she swam until her limbs grew heavy. At least her body was exhausted now, and her mind was definitely quieter.

Her heart still ached.

She buried her face in the soft fluffy cotton and scrubbed at her damp hair. Her skin was already dry--silver lining of the desert air.

Arms slid around her from behind. Austin nuzzled her neck and murmured her name. She leaned back into his embrace, savoring the feel of his lean hard body against hers. Her head dropped back onto his chest, and she looked up at him in the twilight glow.

"You're back. I was worried about you." Longing whispered through her.

He pressed light kisses along the column of her throat. "I'm sorry. I'm sorry about everything. We need to talk." His deep husky voice held a somber note.

Her throat clenched. Those four words never preceded positive discussions. She should know--she'd broken up with three long term boyfriends the same way. "Okay. Should we go inside?"

He turned her around but kept her in the circle of his powerful arms. "Let's sit outside. Like that first night."

Her lips curved up. "I remember." The beauty of his playing the guitar. The talent in those long artistic fingers. The secrets they'd divulged.

He led her over to one of the lounge chairs. The outdoor lighting illuminated the pool area beautifully, beams of gold spotlighting the date palms and the shimmering water. Her stomach continued its uneasy dance and her hands trembled. Was this the end?

They sat and he angled toward her and took her hands in his. "Let me get this all out first, okay? Questions after."

She nodded. Not a problem. Her usual quick speech seemed to have evaded her.

"First, I'm sorry you had to witness the fight between me and Ryan. I know you're an only child but it's not the first time he and I have gotten angry and said things we don't mean. I was furious he'd just assume the story was true.

"We've always had a dynamic that was almost like he was my dad because before Chris came into the picture, he'd stepped into that role for Grant and me. Anyway, I was a rebellious little shit for years and got into some trouble. Maybe sometimes he forgets I'm thirty now, not a fifteen-year-old delinquent."

"Delinquent?" Somehow she could see him being a mischievous boy, pushing the limits of what he could get away with. But a reckless delinquent?

He held one hand. "Questions later. But yeah, delinquent —skipping school, drinking. I'll tell you some stories one day but not tonight. Anyway, I saw red and felt like all the work I've put in over the last year wasn't good enough. That I'd always only be part of the Hotel Kings because I was Ryan's brother and needed a new career. But we just talked, and we worked it out."

He paused and scrubbed his hands through his hair. When he lifted his arms, a giant bandage covered his elbow, and his hands were crisscrossed with scratches.

She caught his arm and he winced. "Hey, what happened? Why are you all scraped up?"

His lips quirked. "Hold on, I was almost there. Anyway, I needed to ride to clear my head. Call it my meditation. And

I'd figured it all out and was turning into this cute little store to get an ice cream cone and head back when a car almost clipped me and sent me sprawling into some bushes."

"You got in an accident? Oh my god, I told you that bike was a death machine. Are you okay?" Her heart stuttered.

He nodded. "I'm fine. Bruised and a little banged up but nothing serious. The person didn't even stop. The restaurant owner took good care of me, and made me hang out for an hour to make sure I was okay, which I am.

"But I need you to listen because this is important. Can I tell you what I've decided?" His voice lowered.

Her pulse thundered through her veins––she could feel it in her temples. He was leaving. Abandoning the hotel and abandoning her. Every muscle in her body tensed, all her years of mindfulness training out the window. "Go ahead."

He clasped her hands. "I'm staying here and running the hotel. I'm good at it and I love working with my brother and friends. Liam's getting a strongly worded letter to cease and desist and stop spreading lies. I never told him I was return-ing. He stopped by last month out of the blue and I made it clear. He kept trying to reach me, but I didn't call him back. If I'd ever considered playing with him again, his games made that impossible. No way."

She nodded and her shoulders softened. He hadn't lied. And more importantly, he'd shown he wasn't some careless bad boy like she'd initially assumed. He was nothing like the selfish jerks she used to waste her time with, who only wanted her for what she could give them. He was the first person in her life who gave her unconditional emotional support. He wasn't leaving.

He took a deep breath. "I know this has all been fast between us, but it's right. I haven't written a word in almost three years since the day Tommy died. And I've been writing again."

"You have? That's wonderful." Her heart warmed.

"It's because of you. Being with you inspires me. Being with you makes me happy. Your inner strength, your bright light, your compassion…so many things about you just draw me in and make me never want to leave. I'm in love with you, Kenzie." His eyes gleamed in the evening light.

Joy filled her. "Austin, you're like this beautiful artichoke and with every layer you shed, you show more of your beautiful, kind soul. I've never felt like this about anyone before. I thought I had a foolproof plan for my future. I didn't expect you."

He threw back his head and laughed, then scooped her up onto his lap. "You're saying I wasn't in that fancy laminated business plan you gave me, under a green tab labeled 'fall for my hot boss'?"

She wrinkled her nose at him. "Laugh all you want. My fall for the perfect man plan wasn't scheduled until a few years out. But I didn't expect you to be so incredible. I figured you were just another rockstar leaving broken hearts in his wake. So I tried to fight my instant attraction——"

"Instant attraction, huh?" He growled and caught her chin in one hand, his pupils dilating.

She rolled her eyes. "As if you couldn't tell. Let me finish. I tried to resist you but once I started to see the man beneath the surface, I couldn't help falling for you."

"Falling?" His dark eyes narrowed. "Be more specific."

Heat curled down her spine and a surge of power filled her. This amazing man loved her and wanted her more than anyone had in her life. But he'd just scared her by running off, so she'd tease him a little bit before she said three words she'd never uttered to a man before.

She wound her arms around his shoulders and pressed a kiss against the powerful column of his throat. "More specific?"

He slid his hand to the back of her head and slanted his mouth against hers. "Kenzie. Give me the words." He deepened the kiss, his tongue danced and swirled with hers, his minty breath mingling with hers.

She pulled back a few inches and met his hooded gaze. "I love you Austin Michaels."

His smile was triumphant. "I love you Mackenzie Banks." He captured her mouth again. The hot desert evening wrapped around them like an embrace and she melted against him, savoring their closeness. Savoring this man.

Too soon, he lifted his head. "I have something for you."

"Don't stop kissing me. You're all I want."

His chest rumbled. "I wrote you a song. Let me play it for you. Then we'll go inside, and I'll let you have your way with me."

"A song? You wrote me a song?" Her heart took a long, slow roll in her chest.

He pressed a kiss to the tip of her nose and set her aside. "I told you I've been writing lyrics again. They're all about you. About us."

He picked up the guitar she hadn't noticed and placed it across his lap. He glanced down for a moment, strumming a few chords before lifting those heartbreakingly beautiful eyes to hers.

"It's called *Complete*. And it's for you, my love."

Elation coursed through her. "I love you."

He began to sing.

EPILOGUE

The Monroe, Opening Gala, September

Austin double-checked the podium's compartment to confirm his guitar was there, then tapped the microphone, eager to give the opening night speech, then move on to the good part.

The crowd quieted and focused on him. Uncharacteristic nerves skated down his spine and sweat prickled on the back of his neck. And not from the heat lingering in the early twilight air. Kenzie's sea siren gaze found him across the clusters of guests and warmth filled his chest. Under the subtle ballroom lights, her hair gleamed golden, and her emerald green dress made her resemble one of the old Hollywood stars they were honoring.

"Hi everyone, I'm Austin Michaels, General Manager of The Monroe, the fourth location of the Hotel Kings' luxury boutique California hotels. We appreciate you celebrating our grand opening with us. Each of our resorts features a special theme, and The Monroe is an ode to old Hollywood when everyone from Bing Crosby to Marilyn Monroe used to vacation in the desert." He waved an arm around to the black and white movie prints adorning the ballroom walls.

The crowd cheered and clapped.

He lifted his champagne flute. "We hope you'll return year after year, just like they did. In addition to our world class restaurant, incredible rooms, and Sanctuary Spa designed by Kenzie Banks, we're offering live acoustic music under the stars. Let's toast to my incredible team and family, without whom tonight wouldn't be happening. No way could I have done it without them. Thanks."

Glasses clinked and applause filled the room once again. The guests turned back to their conversations and Austin cleared his throat––now or never. He grabbed his guitar.

"If you could give me a few more moments of your time, I'd like to play a song. Some of you may know me from my time as a full time musician. I haven't written a song in three years until this one. It's dedicated to Kenzie Banks, the woman who reawakened my muse. I played it for her but I wanted to declare it to the world. It's called *Complete*."

Kenzie's eyes widened and a hush fell over the crowd. The heated air was expectant and heavy.

If he hesitated any longer, he'd chicken out. He strummed the first chords and started to sing,

When we're alone together life is beautiful. A magical world––complete.

Your love, your passion, your hands on me. Nothing and nobody else make me feel so complete...

Their gazes locked and Kenzie crossed the room toward him, her lush lips parted, a flush of pink across her high cheekbones. She stopped in front of the small stage, her arms hugging her slender waist.

After he sang the last note, the fashionably dressed crowd

burst into applause calling out for more. Instead, he placed his guitar down and beelined for Kenzie. He caught her hand and led her out to the patio where they'd sat the first night they met.

Instead of the cheap plastic chairs, elegant cocktail tables and chairs were scattered around the patio. For now, the crowd remained indoors, and he had her to himself. His heart pounded against his ribs and his throat was tight.

"Austin, aren't you supposed to be the host of the party?" Her fingers remained intertwined with his and her voice was husky.

He caught her other hand and turned her to face him. "They're fine for a few minutes. I want to celebrate for a few minutes with you."

"Kiss me, then." She stepped closer, so she was flush against him.

Her peachy scent surrounded him, and the warmth of her body seared into him. "In a minute."

Her brows drew together. "Is everything okay?"

An unfamiliar rush of nerves danced down his spine. "I'll let you know in a minute."

"Austin?"

Now or never. Still holding her hands, he dropped to one knee. "Kenzie, I know it's only been four and a half months since we met, but I feel like we've known each other forever. Like I said in your song, you make me feel complete, like no matter what happens in the world, as long as you're by my side, I'll be happy. You're strong and giving and sweet and so dedicated to being the best person you can be. I know you're the best woman for me and I want to be the best man I can be for you. I love you with every fiber of my being and I want to make it official.

"Kenzie, will you make me the happiest man in the world and marry me?"

Tears rolled down her cheeks and she laughed through the tears. "Yes, yes, yes. I love you so much. I have no doubts you are the best man for me, even though you showed up early. I would be honored to be your wife."

Austin whipped the small velvet box out of his pocket, opened the lid, and offered it to her. The brilliant cut diamond surrounded by pave diamonds sparkled in the evening light.

Kenzie gasped and pressed her hands to her mouth. "It's beautiful."

His hands trembled as he pulled out the ring and slid it on her finger. "You're beautiful. I love you."

"It's perfect and so are you. Now kiss me again, fiancé." She stepped into his waiting arms and lifted her face to his.

His lips curved up and he lowered his mouth to hers. "I love it when you're bossy."

"I'll remind you of that often." She murmured before parting her lips for him.

Much too soon, he lifted his head. "Let's go celebrate, my love."

She threaded her fingers through his and together they returned to the ballroom.

WHAT'S NEXT

Thank you for reading *Palm Springs King*! I hope you loved Austin and Kenzie's story as much as I loved writing it.

If you have a moment, please leave a review for *Palm Springs King* on your favorite book site.

****

Ready for Lucas and Brigitte's Beverly Hills romance?
Beverly Hills King arrives 2024.

ACKNOWLEDGMENTS

I want to thank my wonderful beta readers/critique partners: Joanna Kelly, Sara Martin, Donna Simonetta, and Christy Hovland—your individualized feedback helps me make the stories shine as bright as possible. I appreciate your time and opinions. Big thanks to Lisa Ray for sharing your hotel industry expertise. Any errors in the book are mine. Thank you to Brenda St. John Brown for helping me write the blurb (yes, one more time!)

I'm not sure how writing romance would be possible without the incredible friends and allies I've made along the way. So many of you have impacted me and changed my life for the better, so thank you so much. You know who you are!

To my wonderful editor, Lindsey Faber, thank you for your brilliance! I don't know how I finished books before you. You always know how to make me dig deeper. Thank you to Shasta Shafer for your excellent proofreading. Thank you, Sarah Paige, for this gorgeous cover--you do incredible work.

Last but not least, to Todd for your unwavering belief in me. I love you. And, finally to my furry kids: Lola, Beau, Josie, and Daisy, thanks for providing me daily laughs and all the cuddles.

ABOUT THE AUTHOR

Claire Marti is an award winning and *USA Today* Bestselling author of swoonworthy Contemporary Romance novels set in Southern California, including the Pacific Vista Ranch series and spin-off California Suits series. She lives in San Diego with her husband, silly dog and three clever cats.

Claire started writing stories as soon as she was old enough to pick up pencil and paper. After graduating from the University of Virginia with a BA in English Literature, Claire was sidetracked by other careers, including practicing law, selling software for legal publishers, and managing a non-profit animal rescue for a Hollywood actress.

Finally, Claire followed her heart and now focuses on two of her true passions: writing romance and teaching yoga.